HAPPILY EVER AFTERS

THE FOUR KINGDOMS AND BEYOND

RETURN TO THE FOUR KINGDOMS

HAPPILY EVER AFTERS

A REIMAGINING OF SNOW WHITE AND ROSE RED

MELANIE CELLIER

LUMINANT PUBLICATIONS

HAPPILY EVER AFTERS: A REIMAGINING OF SNOW WHITE AND
ROSE RED

ISBN 978-0-6480801-9-0

Luminant Publications
PO Box 203
Glen Osmond, South Australia 5064

melaniecellier@internode.on.net
http://www.melaniecellier.com

Cover Design by Karri Klawiter

For Deborah
in memory of all the fun we've had as sisters
and in anticipation of all the good times still to come

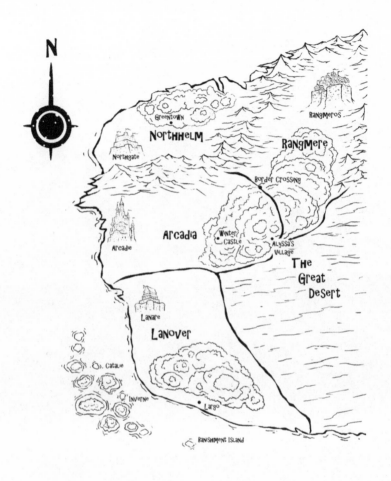

N

Greentown
Northhelm
Northgate
Rangmeros
Rangmere
Border Crossing
Arcadia
Arcadie
Winter Castle
Alyssa's Village
The Great Desert
Lanare
Lanover
Cataue
Inverne
Largo
Banishment Island

ENCHANTMENT

"It wasn't an easy item for me to acquire." The strange man twirled the red jewel through his fingers in a casual manner. "The cost will be high."

"Whatever it is, I'm willing to pay it." The young man eyed the stranger before him with distaste. The man's leathery, wrinkled skin barely looked human. It was almost bronze in color, unlike anything he had seen before in the Four Kingdoms.

"I'm not talking about gold." The short man seemed amused by the younger man's disapproval.

"I will have that jewel, whatever the cost. Just as long as it does what you say it does."

"Of course." The stranger remained unoffended. "I, ah, *acquired* it from a godmother. You've seen its power for yourself. But are you sure you don't want to hear my terms?"

The young man shook his head. His eyes had drifted down and latched onto the gleaming surface of the gem. He didn't bother to look back up. He had already seen a demonstration of the jewel's enchantment, and he knew it was the only way for him to get what should have been his all along.

The many facets of the stone reflected the light until it bathed the entire clearing in a red glow. Still he kept his eyes fixed on it. First, he would claim his rightful place. After that, the possibilities were endless.

He could bide his time. Eventually the perfect opportunity would present itself, and Rangmere would be his to control. He just knew it was his destiny.

The stranger chuckled, but the young man, lost in the red radiance of his dreams, didn't notice.

SARAH

I twirled in front of the mirror and sighed in satisfaction. The pink silk swished around me in a luxurious swirl. It was definitely the most beautiful—and expensive—dress I had ever worn. In the back of my mind I kept calculating the cost of the gown and marveling at the sum. I hadn't grown up in a merchant caravan for nothing.

Thinking about the way the dress complemented my coloring made me think of my cousin. I looked at the closed door and sighed again, this time in exasperation. In another moment, it had changed into a giggle, however. No wonder she was late. It didn't matter that Evelyn's dress would suit her just as well, she was going to hate the pink. I grinned.

Only a royal decree, issued by Rangmere's new queen, had convinced Evelyn that she had to wear a dress instead of her guard's outfit. She had tried to use her new role of personal guard to the queen as an excuse, but Ava had overruled her.

"For this one day, you're off duty," the queen had said. "And I won't hear any more arguing about it."

Even Evelyn had subsided after that. Truth be told, Ava could be a little scary when she put on her royal manner. Sometimes she would get a certain look on her face, sort of cold and calculating, that reminded me she had once used me as a human shield, thrusting me into the reach of several hostile soldiers to cover her escape.

I knew she had changed—was doing her best to keep on changing—but she couldn't entirely erase the person she used to be. I don't think she even wanted to. On some level those attributes were necessary for a monarch, especially a queen. As long as they were properly balanced by a true concern for others.

So, I wasn't scared she would ever do something like that again, to me or to anyone else. But it didn't stop the occasional nightmare, or the shiver I got when she assumed her cold and queenly voice.

I shook off the thought. Ava had only been queen for two days, and Evelyn and I had helped to make that happen. Now was a time for celebration. I was wearing a dress that would have cost my parents an entire month of their earnings, and I looked incredible. I refused to think any but happy thoughts.

I returned to twirling in front of the mirror and imagining the look of horror that would soon be on Evelyn's face. The smile was back within seconds.

I was just wondering how I would ever bear to take the dress off when the door opened.

"Finally!" I turned around to confront the latecomer. But to my surprise it was Mathilde, not Evelyn, who was letting herself into the room.

"Still wearing it?" She smiled at me.

"I can't bear to take it off." I stroked the material lovingly. "How did yours fit?"

"As excellently as I can see yours does. They must have been up all night working on them."

"From what I understand, they had just about every seamstress in the city working shifts. They did a marvelous job."

"Oh, that's right, you talked to the head seamstress, didn't you?"

"Yes, I couldn't risk them putting us in something horrid." I scrunched up my nose at the thought. "I shouldn't have worried though, they'd already picked out the material, and it's perfect. They were friendly, too. The head seamstress is splendid and was even interested in some of my suggestions. The sashes were my idea."

I pointed at the light gold sash that highlighted my trim waist. It was the perfect complement to the deep rose of the dress, and I felt yet another glow of satisfaction. The Rangmeran court wasn't going to know what hit them.

I grinned. "She's offered to work with me to design some dresses when all of the excitement is over, too. I can't wait."

Mathilde glanced at the second, untouched dress lying across my bed.

"I take it Evelyn hasn't found the time to try her dress on?" Mathilde's voice mirrored my own amusement. "Has she even seen it yet?"

"I don't think so." I shook my head. "And don't you dare spring it on her when I'm not around. I have a score to settle with her. You wouldn't believe how she laughed at me yesterday! I think this dress is the perfect way to do it."

The smile crept back onto my face. I knew Evelyn thought I should take life a little more seriously, but I just didn't see the point. If I could simply choose to be happy and see the lighter side of things, why in all the kingdoms wouldn't I?

"I wouldn't dream of it," Mathilde said earnestly.

The Arcadian girl had been a good friend to me in the weeks we had spent as Ava's protectors. Now that Ava had succeeded in winning her kingdom, I wished Mathilde was staying in Rangmeros instead of heading straight back to Arcadie as soon as the wedding and coronation were over.

"You'll need to get back into your regular clothes now,

though," Mathilde continued. "We're all due in the gold sitting room for some sort of official pre-wedding lunch. Apparently, it's a Rangmeran tradition for the bride's party. You'd better bring both dresses. I think we'll all be getting dressed there, too."

With a sigh, I slipped out of the beautiful dress and into my regular clothes.

"I'll be wearing you again soon," I promised the dress as I laid it out on the bed on top of Evelyn's.

When I turned around Mathilde was laughing at me with her eyes.

"Come on, then," she said.

"So, I hear you've already got your eye on a couple of the young noblemen," said Mathilde, as we made our way through the castle.

I laughed. "Who told you that? Evelyn? Ava?"

"That's not a denial." Mathilde raised her eyebrows at me.

I smiled with self-satisfaction. "And why should I deny it? Clearly this court needs to be whipped into shape, and I'm just the girl for the job."

Mathilde chuckled. "Well, that's probably true."

"Of course it's true!"

I was about to launch into a more detailed explanation when we were accosted from a side corridor. Turning, I saw a group of young nobles approaching us. I recognized several of them as the richest and most popular young people at court, but I wasn't familiar with the one leading them. He was tall and broad-shouldered, and with his wavy dark-gold hair, just on the long side of short, he was exactly my type.

I privately admitted that, if I had seen him before, he would have gone straight to the top of my list of attractive Rangmeran men. I would have been astonished to find out that any fewer than half of the girls present were in love with him. And it was immediately obvious that despite his earlier absence, he was the leader of this particular set.

A challenge, then. I smiled.

He glanced condescendingly in our general direction. "We need food and drink brought to the small salon immediately." His tone was imperious and slightly arrogant, and I couldn't help my metaphorical hackles rising.

A challenge indeed, but not the one I had at first supposed. He was immediately transferred from the top of my 'fall in love with' list to the top of my 'teach a much needed lesson' list.

My narrowed eyes must have tipped him off because he gave us a more careful look, dwelling on the pile of fabric in my arms.

"Oh, apologies," he said, "I thought you were servants. We're having the most difficult time finding anyone." He flashed an unconcerned grin that was clearly supposed to melt us into little puddles at his feet.

I remained unmelted.

"Well, it is a rather important day," I said, my tone deceptively mild. "Perhaps the castle servants have something more important to do than wait on you."

He raised both of his brows and looked me over again. "You're two of the Arcadians, aren't you?"

"Arcadians?" I scoffed and turned toward my companion. "Come on, Mathilde, we don't have time for this. Ava is expecting us."

I sailed off down the corridor, trusting that Mathilde would follow me. When I didn't hear her steps, I glanced back and gestured for her to join me. Several of the noble girls were tittering behind their hands, but the mystery man was staring at my retreating form with curious eyes.

When I turned away again I allowed myself a smile. Overall, I felt that had been a success.

"Sarah, really!" Mathilde waited until we'd turned a corner

before tugging on my arm to slow me down. "Was that necessary? Do you even know who that was?"

"That," I said, "was a prime example of why the Rangmeran court is in such sore need of my influence."

Mathilde raised one eyebrow at me, and I burst out laughing. After a moment, she joined in.

"Sorry, Mathilde," I said when we both subsided, "I just couldn't resist. So, who was he?"

"His name is Miles, and he's Lord Adelmar's only son."

She gave me a significant look, and I winced. No wonder the rest of them deferred to him. His family was easily the most powerful family at court after the monarchs. I had possibly bitten off more than I could chew.

I pondered for a moment and then shook my head. I might not be nobility, but I had been handpicked by the queen herself as an attendant at her wedding. How much harm could it really do if I played, just a little, with this particularly handsome and arrogant member of the court?

EVELYN

$\mathcal{I}$ stood at attention before the desk, my spine rigid. The captain of the guard observed me for a long moment without speaking.

"So," he said at last, "you're the new personal guard to Her Majesty."

"Yes, sir." I kept my tone formal.

"You weren't my choice."

"No, sir."

He regarded me for another long, silent moment.

"I would have preferred Her Majesty trusted me with the choice. But there's no gainsaying her, of course. And I'm fair minded enough to admit that you excelled at the Trials."

The Monarchy Trials, where Rangmere chose their new ruler, had been well attended by local dignitaries, but I hadn't realized any of the castle guards were present. I tried to repress an inquiring look.

"Oh, aye." He gave a chuckle. "I was there. You showed yourself to be capable and observant. Two important qualities in a personal guard."

I felt a glow of pride. I had come up directly against Ava's brother, and my pleasure at proving myself against royalty was still fresh.

The captain of the guard shook his head. "His Highness, on the other hand. Well, he was always a little too sure of himself. Didn't believe he could lose. I did my best to train him, and there's no denying he had a natural proficiency." He gave his head another shake. "But he wasn't one of my guards, and there was only so much I could do.

"Hans, however…" His face broke into an unexpected smile.

"You mean His Highness?" I asked, a little coolly. Hans had received the honorary title when he became engaged to Ava.

"Oh, aye, aye, right you are." The captain nodded approvingly. "But I trained him from a lad, and it'll take some getting used to. He was the best trainee I ever had."

He smiled reminiscently. "Almost broke my heart when he took the position of personal guard to Princess Ava, as she was at the time. I'd had my eye on him to take over my position is the truth of it. But turns out he landed on his feet. No surprises there."

He turned a suddenly sharp eye on me. "Don't get any notions, mind you. I run a tight ship, and I won't take any insubordination. I don't know what it's like in those merchant caravans, but personal guard or not, you come under my jurisdiction."

"Yes, sir," I said. "In the caravan, we answered to the Guardsmaster. I'm no stranger to the chain of command, and I assure you I have no desire to subvert it. My only aim is to ensure Her Majesty's safety."

"That's as it should be, and I'm glad to hear you say so." The Captain regarded me for a short moment before heaving a sigh. "It's only fair to warn you that you're likely to meet some resistance from the other guards. They weren't there at the Trials, and you're an unknown with some big shoes to fill. It won't help matters that you're a woman, either. We've had female guards in the past but none at the moment. The men will want to test you, I'm sure."

"Yes, sir."

The Captain watched my rigid bearing with a twinkle of amusement in his eye. "Yes, yes, that's all very well, but you do understand what I'm saying, don't you?"

"Yes, sir." I allowed myself a small smile. "Female guards aren't so common in the caravans, either. It's nothing I'm not used to."

"Ha!" His laugh was more like a bark. "A bit of adversity only makes you stronger."

"Exactly, sir."

He was silent for another moment as he eyed me again.

"Dang it," he said at last, a little explosively, "you impress me, girl! Makes me hopeful that Her Majesty might know what she's doing after all!"

"She usually does, in my experience," I said, my voice dry.

"Oh aye, aye, that she does." He chuckled again. "Well, this will be interesting and no mistake. It'll do my men good, too. It's unsettled times we've been living through, and they could do with a good shake up. You come to me if any of them get too far out of line, though."

"I'm sure that won't be necessary, sir."

"No, no, I daresay not."

He was smiling as he gestured for me to be gone.

Outside his office, with the door firmly closed behind me, I allowed myself to slump a little. It had gone better than I'd expected, but it was still a relief to have it over. I considered my next move.

Ava had insisted that I take the entire day off from my new duties as personal guard, but unfortunately that didn't give me the day off from my responsibilities as a bride's attendant. Reluctantly, I admitted that I had reported in to the captain of the guard to avoid trying on my dress with Sarah. She wouldn't be impressed, but I was trusting that her excitement over the wedding would overrule her annoyance.

I couldn't put it off any longer, though. We were all due at some sort of bridal lunch, and it wasn't the sort of event I could miss. I took off down the corridor, my stride steady. At least the food should be good, and there would be dancing later. So it wasn't all bad.

SARAH

*I*t was no surprise to see Evelyn in the gold sitting
room, still in her guard's outfit and closely shadowing
Ava. She was taking her new role very seriously.

"Really, Eve!" I put my hands on my hips. "Ava already told
you to take the day off. I've been waiting and waiting for you in
my room. We were supposed to try our dresses on so the seam-
stresses could make any last-minute adjustments."

"I was just giving you a longer opportunity to admire yourself
in your dress," said Evelyn dryly. She knew me far too well.

"I was merely following instructions." I raised my nose into
the air. "Something of which you seem incapable."

"Well, I'm here now." Evelyn sighed. "Let's see them."

I had wrapped the dresses in a long length of plain, undyed
cotton, so I carefully laid them down on a handy sofa and
unveiled them. I couldn't help a sigh of admiration as they were
revealed.

"Pink!" Evelyn sighed again. "I should have known."

"Sorry," said Ava, speaking up for the first time. "Apparently
my mother's attendants wore pink, and the head seamstress
thought it would be a nice way to honor my parents."

A brief shadow passed across her face, and I felt a moment of guilt. Today was supposed to be about Ava, not about me. I determined to put the rest of my efforts into cheering her up.

"It's a beautiful thing to do, and they're beautiful dresses," I said. "And for all she protests, Evelyn will look stunning in it."

I looked at my cousin a little wistfully. With her long legs, she managed to make anything look elegant. I often felt she'd gotten a better deal out of our shared genes than I had. And she didn't even appreciate it!

"But none of us will hold a candle to you, Ava," I said, forcing myself back on track. "Have you seen your dress yet?"

Most of the head seamstress' efforts had been focused on the joint wedding and coronation dress that Ava would wear. And somehow, despite the limited time, she had surpassed herself.

"I haven't, actually." Ava looked rueful. "There have been far too many other details taking my attention. It's going to be brought around as soon as we're finished eating. I wonder where the others are."

Even as she was saying the words, the door opened to reveal three slightly nervous looking girls. Two looked to be about my own age, but the third couldn't have been more than fifteen. They were followed by Clarisse. The older princess looked calm and mature next to the others, and I was once again glad that she had decided to stay in Rangmere to support Ava. With her husband, Prince Konrad, dead, she had been offered the option of returning to her home kingdom of Lanover.

Ava greeted the new arrivals enthusiastically and was about to introduce us all when the door opened again. We were overwhelmed by a wave of servants bearing a lavish lunch.

"Goodness!" Ava gazed around in astonishment. "However did the cook manage all this? I would have thought the kitchens busy enough preparing the feast for tonight."

"Don't you worry, Your Majesty," said the housekeeper.

"There will be plenty of food tonight. The castle won't let you down."

We all rushed to load up our plates. We were under stern instructions to eat well since the master of ceremonies didn't want any of the attendants fainting during the ceremony.

The food made the introductions less awkward, and soon the noble girls appeared more at ease. I could hardly blame them for being intimidated by Ava. In fact, the Rangmeran court in general seemed a rather dour and intimidating place. One of the many altruistic reasons I was sticking around. Clearly the court needed me.

"The youngest is Adelmar's daughter, Annabelle," said Evelyn into my ear.

I looked her over curiously. So that was Miles' sister. There wasn't much of a family resemblance.

"I would have expected her to be a little more...poised," I whispered back, thinking of Lord Adelmar's subtle composure.

"Not all parents attempt to fashion their children in their own image, apparently." Her eyes flicked to Ava as she spoke. The new queen had escaped her father's plans for her but only just.

"Perhaps she's naturally shy."

"Perhaps."

The head seamstress arrived before the food had been cleared away, but she refused to unwrap Ava's dress until the servants had returned and removed every remaining scrap of food. Evelyn was clearly impatient with the delay, but I applauded the caution.

When she finally unveiled the gown, there was a collective sigh from the assembled women. My eyes flew to Ava. She was staring at the creation with wide eyes. I smiled. Ava might be tough, but some things were universal. Every girl wanted to look incredible on her wedding day.

After a communal pause, we all rushed forward to help the queen into her gown. The head seamstress held up her hands to stop us.

"I only need one assistant. We mustn't crowd the dress." She gestured toward me.

I glowed with pride to be the trusted attendant.

Within minutes, we had Ava in the dress. Her hair had already been piled up on her head in gentle curls, so I stepped back to admire the effect.

There was another moment of silence that was broken by Mathilde.

"Oh, Ava!" She began to cry.

Evelyn rolled her eyes, but two of the other girls joined in. I settled for a satisfied smile.

The gown looked even more lovely than I had imagined. Made of ivory silk and decorated with lace, embroidery and tiny glints that came from real diamonds, it hugged her torso before blossoming into the fullest of full skirts. It had cap sleeves and a soft sweetheart neckline and the longest train I had ever seen. The overall effect was elegant, somehow both understated and magnificent. Ava looked every inch the queen.

The head seamstress produced a deep purple sash, edged with gold, and showed Ava how to put it on over the dress. She would add the sash for the coronation, scheduled to take place immediately after the wedding ceremony.

Before I knew it, we were being bustled into our own dresses. I was satisfied to see that Evelyn looked as gorgeous—and as unhappy about it—as I knew she would. Evelyn had always preferred looking deadly to beautiful. I shook my head. She underestimated just how effective beauty could be. It was a side effect of trying to succeed in a male-dominated field. Sometimes I felt sorry for her, but strangely enough, she liked her life.

∼

It seemed like only minutes later that we were all gathered in the corridor outside the great hall. The hall was full to bursting with people, members of the court in the front of the room and as many commoners as could fit in the back. The orchestra struck up, and everyone in the room rose to their feet, those on the aisle craning their necks to see Ava.

She looked calm and more at peace than I'd ever seen her. She stepped forward, walking alone, her eyes fixed on Hans, standing at the far end of the room. He was a long way away, but the joy and wonder on his face were still obvious. I smiled in satisfaction. Even Hans, who had been Ava's shadow for years, looked stunned by her appearance. That meant we'd done our job well.

As the only royal attendant, Princess Clarisse walked immediately behind Ava, carrying the end of her train. The rest of us entered behind them, walking in pairs. We'd been arranged by height order, so I took my place at the front with Lord Adelmar's daughter while Evelyn followed at the back.

The combined weight of so many eyes felt a little overwhelming, and I clutched my flowers tightly. I carefully held the happy smile on my face, though. Once again, I represented my people, the traveling merchants.

As we neared the front of the room, I spotted Miles out of the corner of my eye. He was positioned in the second row from the front, next to his father, and smiling at his little sister. I was careful to keep my eyes forward, but I still saw the moment when his gaze moved to me. My peripheral vision is excellent.

His expression changed from friendly encouragement to something I couldn't quite place. There was definitely shock, however. I wasn't sure if he had been unaware I was an attendant or was just surprised to see how well I cleaned up. There was enough admiration in his look for it not to matter much either way.

One of the noble girls who'd been with him earlier in the day sat on his other side. She tugged at his arm to claim his attention.

I quickly transferred my own focus back to Ava and Hans but couldn't help wondering if Miles and the girl were betrothed. It was common practice among the nobles, after all.

~

After the ceremony, the attendants took seats reserved for us in the front row so we could watch the coronation. I wondered how it looked to the people at the back of the room. Could they see how seriously Ava was taking her responsibilities? Could they see how much in love the newlyweds were? From the crowd's tumultuous applause, it seemed like they could.

For myself, I sternly controlled my impulse to glance over my shoulder and see if Miles was looking at me. I wouldn't give him the satisfaction, just in case he was.

When all the formalities were complete, the commoners began to stream from the back of the hall, heading toward the celebration set up for them in the castle courtyard. The nobles, however, were all eager to express their congratulations and assure the new monarchs of their loyalty.

Mathilde had disappeared, no doubt in search of Aldric, so I grabbed Evelyn's arm and indicated with my head that we should make our way through the press of people and out of the room.

She looked reluctant, but I rolled my eyes at her and leaned forward to yell above the noise.

"You're off duty today, remember? And there are plenty of guards here keeping watch over the queen. Stop worrying and enjoy yourself!"

She shrugged and nodded her agreement. Together we struggled to our feet and began to make our way through the crowd. I was so hemmed in that it was all I could do to keep sight of Evelyn, and I was afraid that someone was going to step on my dress and tear it. I was just skirting around a particularly large gentleman, when I felt a tug at the back of my head.

I whirled around, but whoever had touched me was gone, swallowed by the throng of people. I patted my hair, checking that it was all still in place, and realized that one of the pale pink roses had fallen from the arrangement. I looked down but could see barely a foot around me in any direction. I resigned myself to the knowledge that the flower had certainly been crushed by now. It was a good thing the official part of the day was over. After all, I had every intention of dancing so hard that all of my roses might be gone by the end of the night.

The thought put a smile on my face, and Evelyn's hand appeared between two faceless members of the court and tugged me free. I breathed a sigh of relief and thanked her.

The back of the room had been cleared by this point, so we were able to make our more leisurely way out of the room and toward the reception. I did a little skip and ignored Evelyn's disapproving glare.

"We did it, Eve," I said. "We won the kingdom. Hans and Ava are married and crowned and everyone who needed to be was properly impressed. On days like this, I can't help but think that maybe we really are as good as we think we are."

Evelyn laughed and shook her head at me. "I'm glad you're sticking around, little cousin. Rangmeros wouldn't be the same without you."

"Little?" I raised one eyebrow at her. "I'll remind you that I'm actually three months older than you!"

Evelyn just laughed again. "So, have you narrowed down which of the noblemen is going to be your victim?"

I knew she was only joking, but I couldn't help a small blush.

"Oh, ho! Tell me more!"

She looked entirely too delighted, so I resolutely shook my head.

"What about you, Evelyn? Seen any guards that take your fancy?"

She snorted, and not even my perceptive eye could pick out a faint flush. I figured it was probably a good thing since I'd already spotted the perfect young nobleman for her. She'd scoff at the idea of being courted by one of the nobility, so I'd have to tread carefully. I didn't doubt my abilities though, and the young man in question seemed perfect.

"Alright, that's enough of that," said Evelyn, bringing me back to reality. "I want no part of whatever you're scheming. And don't look all innocent at me. I know you too well. What we need is some good food and maybe a dance or two to get your mind off it."

"Perfect," I said, surprised to find that, despite our delicious lunch, I was ravenous again.

The entire kingdom seemed in the mood to celebrate, and it was all too easy to be swept up in the light-hearted atmosphere. I ate as much as I could hold, knowing I would be dancing it all off before the night was over.

And sure enough, I'd barely had time to digest my food before the musicians struck up a dance tune, and a young man appeared asking me to dance. The reception was spread throughout a number of rooms in the castle, and all the doors were thrown wide open. With the courtyard and many of the city squares also filled with revelers, it felt as if the whole city was one big celebration.

I danced with several noblemen, a merchant and at least a couple of servants and had somehow made my way into the entry foyer of the castle before I stopped for a break. I took a drink off the tray of a passing servant before finding a shadowy spot next to the castle doors from which I could observe the revelries outside.

I had been standing there for several minutes when someone slipped up beside me.

"We meet again, merchant girl."

I stiffened and glanced back into Miles' golden-brown eyes. My breath hitched slightly. In the flickering light from the bonfire outside, he looked mysterious and alluring.

I once again felt out of my depth.

"I see you've worked out who I am," I said, forcing my voice to stay light.

My eyes flicked over his shoulder to where several of the noble girls from earlier were huddled together watching us. They didn't look happy.

Miles, however, ignored them, keeping his intense gaze on me.

"Of course," he said. "You're the prettiest girl here, and I always know who the prettiest girl is."

There was laughter in his voice, but I wasn't sure if it was aimed at himself or at me.

"Dance with me?" He held out his hand.

I ignored it.

"And you're Lord Adelmar's son," I said, trying to resist his undeniable appeal. "I don't know if I want to get involved with Lord Adelmar's son."

"No." He moved a step closer. "Tonight I'm just Miles. I've heard a lot about you in the last few hours, merchant girl, and I want the chance to find out how much of it is true."

He reached into his breast pocket and drew out a pale pink rose. It looked familiar. He flashed me a grin and twirled it between his fingers before slipping it back into his jacket.

I stared at him, considering.

After a long, silent moment, I placed my hand in his, giving him my most charming smile. "Only the good bits are true, of course, but I'll let you find that out for yourself."

"I look forward to it."

He smiled down at me and led me back into the whirling dancers.

EVELYN

I've always loved to dance. It's such an entirely physical activity. It reminds me of the sword exercises I used to do when I was young, before I'd won enough respect to find a sparring partner. I would have preferred not to be dressed in pink, but there was no getting around a royal decree. I just hoped that the majority of the guards didn't recognize me as Her Majesty's new personal guard. I was going to have a hard enough time earning my place as it was.

My first partner was a young footman, tall enough not to be intimidated by my own height. He was a beautiful dancer, but I didn't let myself get entirely swept away. Staying alert was second nature at this point.

Sarah was right about Ava—for tonight, at least, the queen had enough eyes on her. She didn't need me. My cousin, on the other hand, was a little too likely to lose her head at an event like this.

To be fair to her, I trusted that she could look after herself in the social game she seemed determined to play with the younger members of the court. It was the older courtiers that concerned me. In the single day that had passed between Ava winning the crown and the coronation, I had already seen just how calculating some of them could be. I didn't want anyone deciding that their next pawn would be the young merchant girl who was such a good friend of the queen.

So, I subtly steered my partner through the dance, keeping one eye on Sarah as she danced with one of the young noblemen. As she moved from partner to partner, I shadowed her through the rooms. When nothing untoward appeared, however, I relaxed my vigilance and began to observe the celebrations more broadly.

The majority of people seemed genuinely delighted at the joint coronation and wedding and were throwing themselves into the festivities wholeheartedly. For this one night, the social divide had disappeared, and people danced with whomever they happened to grasp hands. I could hardly blame them after the brief but repressive rule of Ava's brother.

But the true state of things would only be known once the celebrations were over. And I knew firsthand how some men resented having a young woman in charge. Having Hans as king would help. He was well respected among the people. The captain of the guard wasn't alone in viewing Hans as a hero. It was the nobles I worried about. To them, he was still a guard.

I had just ended a dance with a young nobleman, and I hoped he couldn't read any of the thoughts in my face. I smiled up at him and noticed that his focus wasn't on me. He was eyeing a small knot of older courtiers who were half hidden in the shadows of the room. They looked far too serious for the occasion, out of place amid the enthusiastic revelers.

I used my partner's inattention to slip away into the crowd. Working my way as casually as possible across the room, I grabbed a drink and took up a place close to the older men. I was half obscured behind a large plant, but I still kept my gaze on the dancers and a smile on my lips.

"Look at them!" The speaker seemed disgusted by the dancers.

"They love her," said another voice that I didn't recognize. "And how could they not after Konrad's increasing paranoia. I never expected old Josef's son could manage things so badly."

"The prince did seem almost unhinged at the end there," chimed in a third. "But I heard that the godmothers were involved."

There was a general dissatisfied murmur at these words, and I risked a quick glance at the group. I didn't recognize any of their faces.

"Friends, friends," said a fourth voice, much smoother than the rest. "You're looking at this the wrong way. It's an excellent situation and a perfect opportunity for us."

"Ha." There was a bark of laughter. "And how do you figure that, Anhalt?"

I made a mental note of the name.

"Her Majesty is beloved of the people, a great attribute if we are to rebuild our kingdom's strength. And better yet, she is young and inexperienced. She will be looking for guidance and support. And who better to provide such counsel than ourselves?"

I glanced at the group again and saw that most of them were now smiling and nodding. Only one maintained his expression of disapproval.

"That's all very well, Anhalt," he said. "But it's obvious that Adelmar has gotten there first. I've heard rumors he's been offered the position of Chief Advisor."

Anhalt's face assumed an ugly expression. "It wouldn't surprise me. The man is everywhere. It seems to me that it might be time to do something about that."

My eyes, now fixed on the dancers again, narrowed at the coldness in his tone.

"I don't know, Anhalt." It was the dissenter again, and he sounded uneasy. "Adelmar is powerful. Possibly more powerful than the crown."

"What are you saying? That you're against us, or just that you don't have the stomach for it?" Anhalt's voice was still smooth, but there was no mistaking the ice in his tone.

"No, no," said the dissenter hurriedly. "I'll make no move against you. In fact, I'll be the first to congratulate you if you can accomplish it. But I can't risk any part in such a move myself. I have my family to consider."

"Yes," agreed Anhalt, drawing out the word. "I think it would be an excellent idea to consider your family." He paused, and I could almost feel the other man sweating. "Perhaps it would be a good time for you to visit them at your country estate?"

"A…a very good notion," said the other man. "I think I might even leave first thing in the morning. So you must excuse me now, there will be preparations to make."

Out of the corner of my eye, I saw him bow to the other men and then make his way swiftly out of the room.

"Well then, now that we have him out of the way…" said Anhalt.

I pricked up my ears, extremely interested to hear what he would say next, but he never had the chance to continue.

"Gentlemen, gentlemen!" A portly, older man dressed in the finery of a nobleman swept up to the group. He swung his arm in a gesture of welcome, spilling some of the wine out of his glass.

Anhalt shot the newcomer a venomous look, but he didn't seem to notice.

"What are you all doing in here with the dancers? Step outside with me for a breath of air and perhaps a smoke and a nice glass of port, hey?" The drunken man seemed oblivious to the undertones of the gathering he had just interrupted.

Reluctantly the other noblemen separated, some accompanying the portly man outside while the rest dispersed among the dancers.

I cursed to myself. Without hearing any actual plans there was nothing Ava or Hans could do about the disgruntled nobles. They were hardly the only ones hoping to influence the new monarchs. I was sure that this Anhalt had much more sinister plans in mind, but I didn't have a concrete accusation against him.

My eyes lingered on the place where the men had been standing while I considered my options. My gaze was unfocused, so it took me several moments to realize that I wasn't the only one observing the hidden corner. Now that the men were gone, I could see that a younger man was standing along the other wall. He was in the perfect position to have overheard the conversation and, while I observed, he turned and watched Anhalt's progress across the room. It was hard to determine his expression, given the lighting of the room, but he appeared thoughtful.

An ally for Anhalt or for us?

Once Anhalt disappeared, the young man launched himself into the crowd of dancers and was equally quickly lost to view.

I was still wondering about him when I realized I had completely lost track of Sarah. My eyes scanned the dancers, but I could see no sign of her pink clad figure. I sighed and set off for the next room.

I made it all the way to the entry foyer before I caught sight of her again. She seemed to be having a break from dancing while she watched the bonfire in the castle courtyard. I was about to join her and tell her what I'd just overheard when someone else approached her.

I frowned. As I watched their interaction, my frown deepened. When he pulled a pink rose from inside his jacket and twirled it between his fingers, I sighed. I recognized it immediately. It was one of the same roses I was currently wearing in my own hair. And I noticed Sarah was missing several from her arrangement.

When she placed her hand in his and let him lead her into the dance, I retreated to the edge of the room, biting on my lip. I could read her well enough to know that this must be the young nobleman who had made her blush earlier. And he was Adelmar's son. That meant Sarah had just placed herself in the middle of whatever storm was brewing.

I swore aloud this time.

SARAH

*M*iles, it turned out, was an excellent dancer, and when he refused to relinquish my hand after our dance, I let him keep it for another. I had planned to play a little harder to get, but Miles was both good looking and charming, and it was altogether too satisfying to see the eyes of the other girls following us around the room.

Being so close to Ava gave me a certain position, but Miles was giving me an altogether different sort of credibility, and I wasn't about to turn it down. I might have let him have a third dance if I hadn't happened to catch sight of Evelyn across the room.

She was leaning against the wall and watching us closely, a concerned expression on her face. For all her dour ways, I knew my cousin well enough to recognize that something was wrong. Something much more serious than being forced into a pink dress and paraded before the kingdom.

I excused myself to Miles, probably nonsensically since I wasn't listening to what he was saying and hurried over to Evelyn.

"What, done already?" she asked, raising one eyebrow at me.

My stupid cheeks betrayed me for the second time that night with a warm flush.

Evelyn rolled her eyes at me and gestured toward the door. "Come on, I've got something I have to tell you."

As we left the foyer, I turned my head for a last glance back at Miles. He was still standing where I had left him, watching us go with an expression that was half smile, half confusion. I restrained my own smile until I'd turned back to face forward again. Perfect.

Evelyn caught sight of my expression and glanced back as well. I expected another eye roll, but instead her look of concern deepened. Something was definitely wrong.

Before I could ask her what it was, she suddenly clutched at my arm.

"There! That man. Do you recognize him?"

I tried to follow her eyes, but since the entire room was full of people, I had no way to distinguish who she meant.

"Who?" I asked.

"There. Wearing the black."

"Evelyn! You're hopeless. This room is full of men, and at least half of them are wearing black. Could you give me a little more detail?"

Would it kill the girl to describe him a bit more closely? She could probably tell, just by looking at him, how likely he was to beat her in a fight, but I knew she would struggle to describe his outfit even when she was looking directly at it.

"Never mind," said Evelyn. She sounded disappointed. "He's gone now."

"Well, hurry up then, let's get out of here. I want to hear what's going on." Now it was my turn to lead us through the dancers.

Ava and Hans had already retired for the night, so no one was likely to remark at our doing the same. Evelyn had been given a nice room, but it was attached to Ava's royal suite, so I led the way to my rooms. I was still in the guest suite I had been assigned when we arrived, but I was hoping Ava would let me stay there more permanently.

The whole castle was buzzing, so I couldn't be sure we were alone until I had closed the door behind us.

"Alright, Evelyn, what in the kingdoms is going on?" I flopped down onto one of the sofas and kicked off my shoes with a sigh of relief. I was genuinely concerned by Evelyn's behavior, but at the same time it felt so good to be sitting down after so many hours of standing and dancing. I couldn't help releasing a sigh of relief and stretching my arms over my head.

Evelyn sat down on one of the chairs across from me, her body tense and her face abstracted. Of course, she was much more used to being on her feet for long periods than I was.

When she remained silent, I sighed again.

"Evelyn?" I emphasized every syllable and her attention snapped back to me.

"Sorry, it's been a long few days." She rubbed her hand across her face, and I instantly felt guilty. After all, she'd had a much more active role in helping Ava win the crown than I had. She would certainly still have bruises.

"What's going on?" I asked again, but this time in a much gentler voice. Evelyn always looked so unflappable that it was easy not to notice when she was tired or sore.

It didn't take her long to tell me everything she had seen and heard during the celebrations. As soon as she'd finished, I leaped to my feet.

"We have to tell Ava and Hans," I said.

Evelyn just raised her eyebrows and threw an amused look toward my door.

"Not now, obviously!" I said, rolling my eyes.

I met her gaze and couldn't keep a giggle from escaping. She smiled back at me, her eyes crinkling with a silent laugh. Not even Evelyn was brave enough to interrupt Ava and Hans on their wedding night.

"I meant in the morning."

"I'll tell them, of course, when I get the chance. But what exactly do you think they're going to be able to do about it?" She shook her head. "Excuse me, Your Majesties, but some nobles whose names I don't know are annoyed that you've chosen to be advised by Adelmar instead of them. Oh, and another man, whose name I also don't know, was listening to them talk about it."

I sat down again with a groan. "I'll admit it doesn't sound very actionable when you say it like that. Ava just needs to find out who they are and what they're planning, perhaps Aldric and Mathilde…" I trailed off remembering the truth before Evelyn spoke it.

"Aldric and Mathilde are returning to Arcadia tomorrow."

The two Arcadians were the intelligence contingent of our little group, but surely the Rangmeran crown had some sort of intelligence network. But Evelyn continued before I could voice the thought.

"I'm sure there must be a royal spymaster, but it will take Ava a while to determine whose loyalties she can trust. Even among her spies. I just wish I'd been able to overhear a bit more."

I could hear the frustration in her voice and wondered if the new role was overwhelming her. She was usually calmer than this.

"Well," I said decisively, "we'll just have to find out more ourselves. I can…"

Evelyn cut me off. "That's what worries me most. I can see you've already got yourself entangled with Adelmar's son, and I don't want them deciding you're a convenient tool in whatever plot they want to hatch against Adelmar."

"Really, Eve!" I threw her a wounded look. "Entangled? What's that supposed to mean?"

MELANIE CELLIER

She groaned and sank back into her chair. "Trust you to fixate on that part of what I said."

"He is handsome, though, isn't he?" I couldn't help another giggle slipping out.

Evelyn gave another groan and then flashed me a reluctant smile.

"Yes, Sarah, he's very handsome. Although a touch short for my taste."

"Well, that's a relief," I said brightly. "Now is not the time for us to start fighting over men."

"Wow," said Evelyn, "you must be in love. You've only known him for a few hours, and already you're willing to choose him over me."

I gasped. "Evelyn! You know that's not true. Family always comes first." I was about to continue my reassurances when I saw the laugh in her eyes and realized she was teasing me.

"Oh, you, you…" I threw one of the sofa cushions at her when I couldn't think of a fitting word.

She laughed at me, and it was good to see that she'd regained her equanimity.

"In all seriousness, though, Sarah," she said when her laugh subsided. "It's not a good time to be getting involved with Adelmar's family."

"Really, Evelyn," I said, "you should have more trust in me."

EVELYN

*W*ith the kingdom emerging from such a period of turmoil, a royal honeymoon had never even been considered. Ava and Hans were back on duty the morning after the wedding, and I made my report to them about what I'd overheard. Hans was ready to confront Anhalt himself, but Ava gave him such a stern look that he subsided.

"I appreciate your protective instincts," she said with an affectionate smile. "But you're my king now, not my personal guard. This sort of intrigue is part of the job description of being a monarch. We can't overreact."

She sighed. "I haven't had many dealings with Anhalt, but I can't say I'm entirely surprised. It was his uncle, not his father, who was the last count. The two were twins and died at the same time. It was some sort of carriage accident, if I remember correctly. After their death, Anhalt came forward with evidence that it had actually been his father who was the elder twin. I only remember it because it sounded like such an unlikely story. He must have been convincing, though, because he managed to satisfy the Magistrate's Guild. He was awarded the title, and he's been lying fairly low ever since."

"A strange story indeed," said Hans, thoughtfully. "And clearly an ambitious man."

"Yes, exactly," said Ava, nodding. "There were rumors of enchantment and bewitchment at the time, but there was never any proof of it."

"Bewitchment?" Hans looked uneasy. "That's just what we don't need right now."

Ava shrugged. "My father attributed the whispers to spite and jealousy, and he was probably right. And if any proof of such a thing were to emerge, I can always call on my godmother for assistance. But I won't call her for nothing more than a rumor. For the moment, we'll simply have to keep an eye on him. I'll warn Adelmar, of course, but there's not much else we can do at this point." She turned to me. "If you manage to identify any of the other men involved, let me know, Evelyn."

I nodded my agreement, and the royal couple began to talk of other matters. When a delegation of guild leaders arrived for a scheduled meeting, I took my assigned place behind Ava's chair. It was going to be a long day.

I turned out to be wrong. It wasn't a long day; it was a long week.

It seemed everyone of any influence in Rangmeros wanted a meeting with the new king and queen, and it meant I spent all day, every day, standing behind Ava's chair. At least, it gave me plenty of opportunity to learn about the politics of the court and, just as importantly, a chance to identify the men from the conversation I had overheard.

I didn't see them together again but, with the exception of the dissenter, who had presumably returned to his family estate, they did all appear at one time or another. Each time it happened, I took careful note of their name and then informed Ava or Hans after they had departed. It seemed ominous to me that they gave no public sign of any sort of connection or alliance with each other, but there was nothing any of us could do.

The only bright spot in the meetings was seeing Lord Adelmar at work. He was often in attendance in his new role as Chief Advisor, and he was clearly both skilled and influential. I began to hope that Anhalt was out of his depth when it came to the older nobleman.

Although I kept an eye out, I saw no sign of the other observer. He had been significantly younger than the other men, and I wasn't at all sure that he was even a nobleman. He certainly didn't turn up at any meetings with the new monarchs.

After a full week of meetings, Ava and Hans retreated to the vast royal suite for a well-deserved day off. When Hans told me in no uncertain terms that my services would not be required, I couldn't help grinning at him. I was a little relieved when he grinned back.

I spent the morning cleaning, inventorying and supplementing my various weapons and outfits, but I was longing to do something more active. I'd never been so still for so long. It was almost enough to make me regret taking on the position of personal guard.

I considered going in search of Sarah to suggest we go for a ride but found myself grimacing at the idea. Sarah had spent the last week completely swept up by the court, deep in some sort of game with Adelmar's son. It wasn't the kind of game I had ever enjoyed playing, and I was still a little worried for her. She, however, seemed to be having a fabulous time.

And mostly I'd been more than usually inclined to listen to her prattle about the court because I was still hoping to glean some relevant piece of information about the potential conspiracy. Plus, it was interesting to hear her stories of the younger courtiers and to match their personalities with those of their parents who had come for meetings with Ava and Hans.

Unfortunately, in the last couple of days, Sarah had begun to drop hints about a particular young nobleman who had caught her eye. Apparently, she had decided he would be a perfect suitor for me and had adopted the role of matchmaker.

No. I shook my head decisively. *If I hunt down Sarah, she'll drag me along to some court function and try to introduce me to this noble fool she's got lined up for me.*

Naturally I had no idea if he actually was a fool, but it seemed depressingly likely.

What I really needed was a good training session. But I was honest enough to admit I'd been avoiding the training grounds. Or, more accurately, the other guards.

Ah well, I thought, *I'll have to face them sometime.* Plus, I didn't want the captain of the guard to hear of my absence and think it was caused by fear.

Once I'd changed into my practice gear, I headed toward the area of the castle grounds reserved for the guards. I'd seen them training through the windows several times and had longed to be out there, stretching my muscles.

When I arrived at the main training ground I was gratified to find it almost empty. A group of young trainees had just finished a session, and they stared at me as they filed back toward one of the guardhouses. I ignored them.

Piling my equipment on the ground, I began my warm up routine.

"I haven't seen you around here before."

I started, so absorbed in my stretches that I hadn't noticed the man approach.

"I'm new." The words came out shorter than I'd intended. I turned to look at him and had to repress a gasp.

His eyes twinkled at me while his mouth curved into a smile. "That much I gathered."

It was the other observer from the night of the wedding! No wonder I hadn't seen him among the nobles—he was a guard. I was still staring at him, and his friendly smile changed into a look of curiosity.

I quickly gave him a reluctant smile and offered him my hand. I still wasn't sure why he had been observing the impromptu meeting, but I didn't want him to know that I recognized him.

"I'm Evelyn." If he didn't know who I was from my name, I didn't see any need to enlighten him.

"I'm Jake." His grip was firm and his expression friendly. "I don't think I've seen a woman out here before."

I shrugged. "As I said, I'm new."

Like me, Jake was dressed in the casual clothes that marked him as off duty. But there was no mistaking his occupation. He carried himself like a guard and, despite my misgivings, I found the familiar bearing rather comforting. I wondered how I'd missed it the other night.

And whatever his intentions had been at the celebrations, now at least he was showing no inclination to throw stones, physical or metaphorical at me.

My lips curved upward again at the thought of the caravan boys who used to do exactly that whenever they caught me training. I hadn't been amused at the time, but the years had softened the memory. Many of those boys had grown up to be my companions in the caravan guard, and my success in winning them over gave me confidence that I would eventually do the same with the palace guard.

Jake raised an inquiring eyebrow, and I had to repress a flush of embarrassment. He probably thought I was smiling at him!

I shook my head and quickly resumed my warm up.

Jake fell into place beside me, joining in the exercises without comment. We were just completing the last of our stretches when a small group of guards entered the training grounds from the other side. They began to pair up in obvious preparation for sparring practice when one of them noticed us across the yard. He pointed us out to his companions, and I heard a surprised murmur sweep through the group. I was too far away to hear the actual words, though, and the men quickly returned to their own activity.

With my warm up completed, I hesitated. I glanced at Jake, wondering what he intended to do next, but he just stood there, watching me curiously. Moving slowly, I buckled on my practice sword and then hesitated again.

My instinct was to begin the series of individual sword exercises I used to train with in my youth. They were a useful tool to allow a lone swordsman to maintain fitness. And it was what I'd been planning to do when I arrived at the empty yard. But I also knew that I would never have hesitated to join the other guards if I'd been back with the caravan.

Don't be a coward! I told myself firmly and started across the grounds.

Once again, Jake mirrored my actions.

"Where did you train?" he asked, his manner just as open and friendly as before.

"With Caravan Hargrove. I was one of their caravan guards until recently."

Jake gave a quiet whistle. "You must be good, then." He stated it matter-of-factly.

I glanced at him with curiosity. I hadn't expected him to recognize the name of my old caravan.

He shrugged. "Everyone knows the Hargrove Guardsmaster is the best among the merchant caravans. Although I'd wager our own Captain could give him a beating."

I just smiled. Any of the other caravan guards would have hotly refuted this assertion, but I had always found the male need to champion their own turf rather amusing. I couldn't see how it mattered who would win in a fight between the Rangmeran Captain of the Guard and the Caravan Hargrove Guardsmaster. Both men were excellent at their jobs, and both had accepted me as a guard. As far as I was concerned, that was all that mattered.

Jake had paused, as if waiting for my cry of protest. When I said nothing, he continued. "The Guardsmaster wouldn't have offered you a job unless he thought you were one of the best merchant guards around. There would have been plenty of others happy to take the position, I'm sure."

"True enough." I shrugged. "I was raised in Caravan Hargrove, though, so I'm sure that gave me an advantage."

Jake raised an eyebrow again. "A female guard and modest to boot! I would have expected an overabundance of confidence."

When I threw him a mild glare, he raised both his hands and laughed.

"Just to balance out all the male machismo constantly surrounding you."

"Of course," I said dryly. But after a moment I couldn't help smiling. "It can get a bit much sometimes."

He grinned at me. "I can imagine. I don't know what brings you to Rangmeros in general and the castle in particular, but you won't find it any better here. We're just as bad as the next lot I'm afraid."

So, he didn't know who I was. I wondered if he would treat me differently when he found out what I was doing at the castle. Or perhaps he already knew and was just pretending ignorance. After seeing him at the royal celebrations, I was on edge.

But I also had to admit that I found his cheerful demeanor appealing. He certainly seemed nothing like Count Anhalt. In fact, his friendly warmth was at complete odds with the nobleman's cold scheming. I tried to think of a way to prove he had nothing to do with the treacherous noblemen without asking outright. Nothing came to mind.

While I was thinking, we arrived at the group of guards. Slowly the men broke off their practice to stare at me.

"Hello," I said when it became clear no one else was going to say anything. "Mind if we join you?"

"Join us?" The speaker sounded incredulous.

"We don't fight women, wouldn't be a fair fight." There was amusement in the voice of the second guard, but somehow it sounded nothing like Jake's light-hearted humor.

I stiffened, and my eyes narrowed. "Probably true enough," I said, keeping my voice light and shrugging my shoulders. "I'd hate to dent one of Her Majesty's prize guards. But this is the first I've heard of Rangmeran guards turning coward."

A shocked gasp ran through the group, and Jake raised both eyebrows at me. I ignored him.

"Coward, do you say?" The first speaker stepped forward aggressively. "I'll show you who's a coward."

I drew my practice sword. "One on one, standard practice bout."

The rules of a standard practice duel forbade the drawing of blood, which was hard enough to do anyway with the dull practice blades. Instead the match would end when one of us disarmed the other or managed to land a blow that would have been disabling with a regular blade. In a normal training situation, such blows were softened, but I felt sure that my opponent would put his full force behind any blow he managed to land.

I'd better make sure he doesn't touch me then, I thought grimly.

The rest of the guards formed a loose circle around us while we both fell into a preparatory crouch.

One of the watching men called a start to the bout, and my opponent was quick to attack. I blocked him instinctively, falling back and carefully assessing his form and tactics.

When I continued to parry, dancing out of his reach immediately afterwards instead of responding with an attack of my own, he grunted in frustration and increased the tempo of his strikes.

After several minutes of this sort of back and forth, I was confident that I had his measure. He was slightly taller than me and significantly heavier, but he was also a bit slower and lacked the finesse of the better caravan guards. For Ava's sake, I hoped he wasn't an example of the best of the royal guards.

Shifting gear, I went on the attack. My opponent was caught off guard and fell back before my blade, parrying my strikes recklessly. There was no question as to who was the more skilled swordsman, and I was confident it would take me only moments to land a winning blow.

The man's movements had carried us right up to the edge of the ring of watching guards, and as I lunged forward, preparing to finish the bout, one of the men thrust his foot into my path. Clearly, he thought me too focused on my attack to notice and expected to send me tumbling to the ground.

But the caravan boys and their stones had long ago taught me to always keep one eye on my surroundings. At the last possible second, I leaped over the out-thrust foot and drove my blade home.

"Bout," I said calmly, the tip of my sword resting above my opponent's heart. I wasn't even winded.

He stared at me in shock, his face twisted in rage. It took him several long seconds to master himself enough to speak. The delay gave me time to register that the mood around us had the potential to turn ugly. But when my opponent did finally open his mouth, another voice cut in before he could spit out whatever insult he was planning.

"Well, that was illuminating." It was Jake who spoke, and his simple words held an unmistakable tone of menace.

No one replied, but there was the sound of shuffling feet, and I noticed that many of the guards were carefully avoiding Jake's gaze. And despite the simmering anger still evident in several pairs of eyes, including those of my opponent and the man who had attempted to trip me, no one directed any comments my way.

That's interesting, I thought. *I wonder if he's an off-duty officer.*

"We seem to have a talented swordswoman in our midst." Jake directed his eyes back toward me and the warmth returned to them. "I realize we've hardly shown ourselves in the best light so far, but would you consider another bout?"

"With you?"

"If you're game." His smile took any potential sting out of his words.

I looked around the circle and then shrugged and nodded my assent. Despite my win, these men didn't like me, so I really didn't have anything to lose.

Jake drew his own practice sword and stepped into the circle of onlookers.

My previous opponent had melted back into the crowd, but I took careful note of his location, resolving not to allow myself to travel anywhere near him during this bout.

Jake was much slower to attack than the previous guard, but it took considerably less time for me to assess his skill. He was a far superior swordsman. His movements were quick and graceful, and he outmatched me in both speed and strength.

I grinned. There were things the palace guard could teach me after all.

My competitive instincts rose to the challenge, and I knew I was fighting much more skillfully than in the previous match. And yet, I couldn't help but wonder if Jake was prolonging the bout on purpose. Testing me, perhaps, or simply giving me a chance to practice.

After ten minutes of hard fighting, Jake snaked his sword under my guard and lightly tapped my stomach. We both fell back, smiling and breathing heavily, and I felt certain he could have ended the bout much earlier, if he had chosen to do so. I wondered again if he was an officer. Whatever else he was, he was a master swordsman. I suspected he could have beaten my old Guardsmaster from the caravan.

And as I stood there, catching my breath, I realized that Jake had orchestrated our conflict to ensure we never came near any of the watching men. I felt grateful for this sign of his consideration.

My emotions were tugging at me, telling me to trust him, but I kept picturing his thoughtful face as he watched Anhalt walk away through the crowd. I was in unfamiliar territory in court, and I would do well to watch my back.

The rest of the guards seemed somewhat cheered by my defeat, and several even gave me cursory nods. I hoped I had performed well enough to win some respect. I knew from experience that respect was a base I could build from—as good a beginning as any.

Still, it seemed like a good moment to withdraw, so I thanked Jake for the fight and headed straight back to my room in the castle.

I'd barely had time to clean myself up and change out of my practice gear when Sarah arrived.

"There you are! Where in the kingdoms have you been all day?"

I opened my mouth to reply but didn't get any words out before she continued.

"Oh, never mind. Who cares about today, it's tonight that matters." She was practically bouncing on the balls of her feet, her eyes shining at me.

My heart sank. "Out with it then," I said, with a sigh. "What's happening tonight? I can guess from your overabundance of enthusiasm that I'm not going to like it."

Sarah's face transformed into a pout. "I do wonder how we can possibly be related sometimes, Eve. And I don't know why you're so set against the court. You haven't even met most of them. A lot of them are quite nice, you know." She gave me a conspiratorial look. "One in particular."

I responded with another sigh. "I have no idea if you're referring to that noble you've been busy stringing along for the last week or the one you're trying to foist onto me." She opened her mouth to reply, and I held up my hands to forestall her. "And I don't want to know. I've spent the week in meetings with Ava, and I've seen firsthand that the only thing the nobles are interested in is what they can get out of their new sovereigns."

Sarah flopped onto my bed and let out a sigh of her own. "You're not being fair to them. They're not all like that. You've just seen the worst of them. And I'm not taking 'no' for an answer. You're coming to the soiree tonight whether you want to or not."

I groaned and sat down beside her. "Do I really have to?"

"Yes." Sarah's voice was firm. "And I don't know what's gotten into you. You never used to dislike parties so much."

I closed my eyes and rolled my shoulders. "You're right, of course. I'm just out of sorts after a run in with some of the other guards."

"Oooh." Sarah was instantly sympathetic. "Were they as bad as they used to be at the caravan?"

"Most of them were. But it wasn't all bad, so I shouldn't be so despondent really. One of them was downright friendly. And you won't believe who he was."

Sarah bounced upright, her eyes trained on my face. "That's intriguing. Tell me, quick."

"It was the mystery man from the celebrations. The one who was also observing Anhalt."

"Oooh, the other spy." Sarah sounded excited at the news.

"Spy might be a bit much," I said dryly. "He's an incredible swordsman, though. I don't know if I've ever fought someone as skilled. He was off duty, but I think he must be one of the guards, possibly one of the officers. His name is Jake."

"Jake." Sarah said the name thoughtfully. "I wonder if Miles knows him."

I raised both eyebrows at her. "*Miles*, is it?"

She lifted her chin in an attempt to look dignified and then quickly burst into laughter. "I only do it because it annoys the other girls so much."

"I thought you wanted an in with the court, not to annoy them," I said.

"Oh, I don't want to get close to these particular girls," said Sarah. "They're the ones who'd never have time for a simple merchant's daughter, however close she is to the queen."

She wrinkled her nose, and I was reminded of her old feud with one of the other girls from our caravan. Winning herself a place and a social position had always been a game to Sarah. It reminded me that we were family—our competitive instincts just came out in very different ways.

"I'll ask around, see if anyone knows this Jake of yours," she said.

"Hardly *my* Jake."

She waved one of her hands dismissively. "I saw your face when you described his fighting skills. Clearly we're going to have to find a way to exonerate him of all suspicion."

She was openly laughing at me now, and I wondered if that meant she was giving up on pairing me off with the nobleman she'd found. Of course, it wouldn't be much better if she started trying to match-make me with Jake. I flushed at the thought.

"Ha, see! I know you too well," she crowed. "Which is how I know that you'll enjoy yourself at the party tonight if you just give it a chance. Ava and Hans are still locked away, so it's going to be a pretty informal affair. Mostly just the younger crowd." She paused to consider. "Of course, we'll still need to look amazing, so come straight to my suite as soon as you've eaten. We're going to need plenty of time to get ready."

Before I could protest, she was gone. I looked at myself in the mirror and shook my head. There was simply no point trying to resist Sarah when she was in this sort of mood. And maybe she was right. Maybe a party was just what I needed.

47

SARAH

I watched Evelyn's face as we stood in the doorway of the ballroom and smiled in satisfaction. I had been right. She was glad to be here.

It was the smaller of the castle's two ballrooms and already largely filled with dancing couples. Just hearing the lively music had Evelyn tapping her feet beneath her full skirts. I knew how much she loved to dance.

Her eyes stayed locked on the dancers, but I dragged her across the room to a small group of nobles standing next to the refreshment table. Miles stood prominently at their center and, after a week, I knew them all.

I introduced them to Evelyn and could tell from her expression that she was matching each one with their parents. Between her attendance at Ava's meetings and my social dealings with the younger nobles, we were getting a good feel for all the members of the Rangmeran court. Which was exactly how I wanted it to be.

Sometimes, in the middle of a dance, or during a particularly exhilarating conversation, my mind would flash back to all the years I'd spent in Caravan Hargrove. No matter how I joked to

Evelyn or Ava, I had never really imagined myself here, in a royal court. But at the same time, I knew that I was better suited here than I'd ever been in a caravan. My only regret had been leaving my best friend and cousin. So, when Evelyn accepted the role of Ava's personal guard, any hesitation vanished. I was utterly determined to carve myself a place here.

While I was thinking, my eyes wandered to Miles' face, and I saw that he was watching me, a half smile lingering around his mouth. I grinned impishly back, wondering how much of my thoughts he was able to guess. Despite our poor beginnings, he'd so far shown himself to be as astute as I'd expect an Adelmar to be. Several times I'd wondered if our initial conversation had been a test of some sort.

The thought only fueled my grin. If it had been a test, I seemed to have passed. Miles had welcomed me into his group, and none of the others dared gainsay him.

Evelyn watched our silent interaction with a veiled expression. I knew she was wary of Miles and didn't want to get involved. She was right, of course. It was a game. I had every intention of using the nobleman to gain the acceptance into court he could so easily offer.

I wasn't quite willing to admit, even to myself, that I might want something else from Miles. He was both the highest ranked and the most influential of the younger nobles, and my aim wasn't set that high.

Evelyn's eyes strayed back to the dancers.

"It looks like you ladies are in need of a dance," said Miles when he saw the direction of her gaze. "And you promised one to me, Sarah."

"Oh, did I?" my forgetful tone was entirely put on, and I could tell from Evelyn's expression that she could tell.

"You certainly did." The twinkle in Miles' eyes suggested that he wasn't fooled, either.

Evelyn smiled, but she was the only one. The other ladies in the group looked very sour indeed, and I had to repress my own smile. Some segments of the castle populace might resent our arrival, but they would soon learn that we were a force to be reckoned with.

Before I could accept Miles' outstretched hand, I noticed a new face among the crowd.

I grabbed Evelyn's arm and hissed, "There he is!" in her ear.

He was one of the lowest ranked noblemen and barely involved with the court. In fact, he seemed like a bit of an outcast, although no one had a bad word to say about him. It was as if he just didn't fit with the rest of the nobles. Possibly it had something to do with the fact that he preferred physical activity over court intrigue. Apparently, he was a skilled swordsman.

In other words, a perfect match for Evelyn.

The grin dropped from her face, and I almost sighed in frustration. She hadn't even seen him yet. Clearly, she was determined to be difficult.

I watched him make his way over toward us.

"Why, hello," he said, his eyes on Evelyn's back.

She whirled around and stared at him in surprise.

My eyes darted between the two of them. "Do you two already know each other?"

He ignored me and addressed himself to Evelyn. "I don't suppose after your defeat earlier, you'd be interested in joining me for a different sort of dance?"

A sudden suspicion darted across my mind, and I quickly poked Evelyn in the ribs. "Of course she would!"

Evelyn didn't even seem to hear me. "What are you doing here?" she demanded of him, apparently too shocked to be polite.

I stood up on tiptoes to whisper in her ear. "This is the noble I was telling you about!"

"Noble?" Evelyn replied at full volume, and I glared at her. So much for subtlety.

"Guilty as charged," said the man, with an easy smile. "Sir Jacques at your service. It seems we're both full of surprises."

Evelyn raised her eyebrows at him.

"I hear you're Her Majesty's new personal guard."

I looked back and forward between them. So, Evelyn hadn't told him who she was. Interesting.

Jacques. Jake. I smiled at how well things were turning out.

Evelyn, meanwhile, shrugged and 'Jake' responded with a laugh.

"Exactly," he said. He held out a hand imperiously. "Now show me if you dance as well as you fight."

I wasn't sure if she actually meant to do it, but somehow Evelyn's hand found its way into his. Miles, who had been watching the interchange with great interest, was quick to snatch up my own hand so that we were led into the dance side by side.

I looked at Evelyn inquiringly and was relieved to see a small smile on her lips.

That settles it, I thought. *Somehow or other I have to prove to Evelyn that Sir Jacques can be trusted.*

"You know I'm generally considered to be both intelligent and charming," said Miles.

"What?" I asked, my focus still on Evelyn and Jake.

"Exactly," he said with a small laugh. "You're not listening to a word I'm saying and you haven't paid me any attention all night."

I turned my attention back to his laughing face. "You're not the only interesting thing in the Four Kingdoms, you know," I said with a laugh of my own. "I was thinking about something else."

"But that's just it." He assumed a hurt expression although the laugh was still lurking underneath. "I'm not used to dancing with women who are thinking about something else."

"Well, I'm sure it's doing you good then."

"You know, there are several girls back at the refreshment table who would love to trade places with you..." His self-mocking smile was back, but I still shook my head at his bound-less confidence.

"Well, you should certainly feel free to trade partners," I said, letting go of my grip on him. "I certainly won't make a fuss."

He didn't let go of my hand or waist. After a moment, I returned his clasp with a satisfied grin.

"I didn't think so."

He shook his head. "What am I going to do with you, Merchant Girl?"

I affected an expression of surprise. "Do with me? Why, nothing at all! If you haven't yet noticed, I'm perfectly capable of looking after myself."

Miles pulled me closer against him and leaned down so that our faces were almost touching.

"But what if I want to do something with you? What if I want to…" his voice trailed off, and his eyes moved down to my lips.

My heartbeat sped up and I suddenly realized that while we were dancing, he'd maneuvered us right out of one of the many open doors that led on to the long terrace.

The noise and lights of the ballroom were just behind us, but for this one moment we were alone beneath the moonlight. My breathing hitched and my mind scrambled for a suitable response.

Miles was just as intelligent and charming as he claimed to be, and I enjoyed every minute that I spent with him. But he was also heir to one of the most powerful titles in court. He was very useful to my attempts to establish myself in court, but I had no serious hopes of a future with him.

Even as I remembered the disparity in our positions, my own gaze drifted to his mouth. I gasped and wrenched myself out of his arms.

"Miles!" I put my hands on my hips and glared at him.

His own breathing had quickened, but at my exclamation, he gave his head a single shake and then flashed me a cheeky grin.

"You can't blame a man for trying."

"Oh, can't I?" I rolled my eyes. "Anyway, we need to get back into the courtroom before Evelyn notices I've disappeared."

Miles offered me his arm with an exaggerated bow.

"But surely she wouldn't be concerned about you, she knows you're with me."

"I think that's what would worry her the most, actually," I said, without thinking.

"I'm hurt!" Miles clapped his hand to his chest as if wounded.

"No, no," I shook my head quickly. "She wouldn't be worried about you harming me. She's just worried about me being caught up in something aimed at your family."

"My family?" Miles' whole demeanor became instantly serious. "What are you talking about?"

I bit my lip, unsure what to say. I was still flustered from our interaction outside, or I would never have slipped up and mentioned the matter at all.

Miles stopped and spun me around to face him, his hands gripping my shoulders. "What are you not telling me?"

I scrunched up my nose and then sighed. The Adelmars were our allies, after all. Maybe I should have told him already.

It only took me moments to tell him the whole story of what Evelyn had overheard at the wedding and coronation celebrations. His expression darkened, and by the end of the tale he was scowling thunderously.

"You've told my father of this?"

I shrugged. "Evelyn reported it to Ava and Hans. I assume they would have passed it on to Lord Adelmar."

"I don't know why he didn't tell me." Miles looked annoyed, but his eyes were focused above my head, so I assumed his anger wasn't directed at me.

"I'm afraid I'm going to have to go," he said abruptly. "Excuse me."

With a quick squeeze of my shoulders, he turned and walked

out of the room. I watched him leave a little guiltily. I hoped I hadn't stirred up too much trouble between him and his father.

"What in the kingdoms did you say to Miles?" asked a snide voice behind me.

I turned to see three of the noble girls who usually hung around him.

"He certainly couldn't get away from her fast enough," said one of the others, and all three of them laughed behind their hands.

Before I could reply, Evelyn appeared at my elbow. "That's strange," she said, "from where I was standing it looked like he spent the whole evening with her. Or perhaps I'm wrong, perhaps you danced with him before we arrived."

She raised one eyebrow challengingly.

Three identical glares were leveled at her, but none of them could think of anything to say. When Evelyn continued to calmly meet their gaze, the first one snorted angrily and then stormed away. The other two were quick to follow her.

I turned to my cousin.

"Thanks, Eve, but I don't need you to fight for me, you know."

"I know." She gave me a wide smile. "But I can't let you have all the fun."

I felt a little heartened by her response. She must have had a good time with Jake. I hated to pull her away, but I also thought it was time we retired for the night. There had been altogether too much excitement already.

I linked my arm in hers and led her around the edge of the ballroom toward the doors that led to the rest of the castle.

"So, Jake is Sir Jacques, hey?" I asked, my voice light and teasing. "What do you have to say about my matchmaking skills now?"

"Sarah!" She pinched my arm. "I'm not interested in him! I don't even know if I can trust him. I haven't forgotten what I saw at the celebrations even if you have."

"Of course I haven't forgotten," I said, indignant. "But I'm sure he wasn't in league with Anhalt or anything. Why wouldn't he have joined them if he was?"

"I don't know why. I don't know anything," she said, her face crinkling with concern. "And that's exactly what worries me. We need to find out some more information, Sarah."

I sighed. "Well, I might have accidentally let something slip to Miles tonight."

Evelyn raised both eyebrows at me. "So that's what that was all about."

I nodded. "He left to confront his father about it."

We had stepped out into the relatively quiet corridor at this point, and Evelyn gave a low whistle that seemed to echo off the stone walls.

"Well then," she said. "I guess we'll have to wait and see what he has to say next time you meet. If anyone's been able to get more information, it will have been Adelmar."

EVELYN

*A*s much as I was itching to find out more about the potential conspiracy against Adelmar and the crown, I was significantly restricted by my duties as personal guard to the queen. I could hardly go off investigating on my own when I was required to accompany Ava at all times.

It was at least a relief to hear, the next day, that she had cleared her morning of meetings.

"I've given a whole week to the nobles and officials," she told me over breakfast. "It's time I got back in touch with the populace."

In the week before Ava's successful attempt to win the crown, we had spent every day mixing with the women who did their washing in the large square at the center of the city. It was a hub of local activity, and Ava had done a lot toward winning the hearts of the people in the hours we spent there.

It had also been an enjoyable escape from the suffocating atmosphere of the castle under her brother's rule. The Square of Fountains was always overflowing with active children, and my only regret was that my new role wouldn't let me join them in our usual game of quickball. I could understand why Ava wanted to return there.

Ava saw the understanding on my face and nodded. "Yes, I thought we could visit the Square again. Do you think Sarah would want to come with us?"

"I think it would do us all good to get out for a few hours," I said firmly. "I'll just tell her it's a royal command."

Ava shot me a wary look but then laughed when she saw the smile on my face.

"Being queen is wearing me down, and it's only been a week." She shook her head. "I used to live like this all the time, back when my father was alive. I hadn't realized how much I'd gotten used to a different way of life in the weeks I was on the run with all of you. I miss it."

She sounded wistful, and I wished there was something I could do to lighten her load. I had been angry and mistrustful of her when we last traveled together, but I had come a long way in my thinking since then. And her poise and patience in the last week had only increased my admiration for her ability to rule.

"Well," I said, making my voice as light-hearted as I could and rolling my shoulders, "when I'm standing behind your chair for the sixth hour straight, I rather miss it, too."

Ava laughed. "Hans always made an excellent statue back when he was my personal guard, and I'm afraid I never gave him much thought. But then I didn't attend nearly so many meetings when I was just a princess."

Her expression turned sympathetic. "He feels bad for you, you know. He told me so yesterday. In fact, he thinks we need to assign a second personal guard, so the two of you can take shifts. I think it's a good idea."

I shook my head. "I wasn't meaning to complain, Ava. I can assure you, I'm up to the job." I had merely meant to make her smile, not to make her question my competency! I felt a little sick. I'd initially doubted that I had the experience for such an important role but, up until now, I'd thought I was performing well.

"Oh no, no, Evelyn!" Ava reached out to touch my arm reassuringly. "Your competence is not in question, I promise you. It's a sensible suggestion regardless of who's in the role. No single person can be vigilant all day, every day. It's simply impossible. Plus, you need time to maintain your training and fitness. I have no idea how Hans managed it all those years. From what he says now, I think he was the only one willing to take the job." She grimaced.

I could hear the sense of her arguments, but Hans had managed it for years. It had only been a week, and already they had seen what I had been afraid of from the beginning—the role was too big for me, my merchant guard training wasn't enough.

"Well, if that's what Hans thinks is best, then you should certainly take his advice," I said, keeping my voice free of emotion. "He's the one with the most experience in the role, after all. But there's no hurry from my perspective. Take however long you need to find someone you trust."

Ava smiled at me warmly. "I'm just glad I have you, Evelyn."

She stood up, brushing off her hands. "Now, why don't you go and drag Sarah out of bed? The guards outside my rooms can keep an eye on me for now. Plus, Hans should be getting back from his run any time now."

Sarah was already up and dressed and as enthusiastic as Ava and I about a morning excursion into the city. Half an hour later, we were riding through the streets.

In what I suspected was a momentary fit of equal parts rebellion and nostalgia, Ava had dispensed with her ceremonial guard. So, it was only the three of us making our way to the Square of Fountains.

I felt a little uneasy with her decision. It made me solely responsible for her safety, and I was still unfamiliar with the city. But we attracted no attention as we rode through the streets, and the gray cobblestones and houses seemed just like they always had before.

Rangmeros, the capital of the kingdom of Rangmere, was a gray, square city, and I had disliked it when we first arrived. I had grown up surrounded by nature, always on the road with the merchant caravan. But, to my surprise, the city was already starting to grow on me. The uniform gray of the stone only served to enhance the splashes of color that accented it. Every window box of flowers or brightly colored dress stood out.

We arrived at the square faster than I expected, and I was immediately swamped with children. I struggled to extricate myself, attempting to explain to them that I was on duty and unable to play today.

But the women called out to us with welcome, and several of them laughed and told me to start up a game.

"We didn't let anything happen to your princess when you visited us before," called out one, "we won't let anything happen to her now that she's our queen."

I looked at Ava and she gestured for me to stay with the children.

"I'll be safe enough here," she said. "Hans played last time, remember?"

She was right, and the memory reassured me that I wasn't failing in my duties. I threw myself into the game, energized by the enthusiasm of the children. It felt like no time at all before the game was over and I was collapsing next to Sarah.

Sarah had also slipped straight back into her old role and was teaching a small group of girls how to plait reeds into armbands. She had decorated hers with flowers, and the girls' gazes were as worshipful as they had been last time we were here.

"Do you really like court better than this?" I asked her,

reaching over and picking up a completed armband. I whirled it idly around my finger.

Sarah paused in what she was doing and regarded me thoughtfully.

"It's not better," she said at last, "just different. I like both." She elbowed me lightly in the side. "It's why I keep you around, you keep me grounded."

"Oh, really," I said, pushing myself to my feet. "I thought it was because you couldn't get rid of me."

"Well, that, too," she said with an impish grin. She groaned as she scrambled to her feet. "One thing's clear at least. I'm going to have to go a little easier on all those refreshments at the balls and afternoon teas and soirees. I think they're starting to take their toll."

"Very true," I said, my face serious. "I'd been meaning to say something…"

She shot me a worried look, and I couldn't help grinning. "But I figured you'd notice yourself seeing as how you've started having to turn sideways to fit through doors."

She took a swipe at me, but I stepped deftly out of her way. "See?" I said, still smiling. "You're getting slow, too."

She rolled her eyes, and I ducked in close enough to whisper in her ear. "You wouldn't want to risk looking less than perfect for Miles now, would you?"

She exclaimed in outrage and tried once again to catch me. I escaped her easily, and she proceeded to chase me around the fountains, much to the amusement of the children who followed behind us, shrieking encouragement to one or the other of us. I eluded her for several minutes, ducking behind fountains and jumping over benches, purely for the entertainment of our audience. She entered into the drama with equal enthusiasm, pretending to be slower than she really was. When I eventually let her catch me, we both collapsed onto a bench, laughing.

"Don't think I didn't notice the blush," I whispered, too quietly for the children to hear. "I hope you're not forgetting who Miles is."

I shot her a warning look, and she met my eyes, her own full of guilt. But Ava approached us before she could reply.

"If you two are quite finished, we should probably get back to the castle now."

I jumped to my feet, but she was smiling so I relaxed.

"As you command, Your Majesty," I said, bowing low.

The children laughed again, and Ava shook her head at me.

We were all still smiling when we left the square. None of us were really in a hurry to get back, so we walked, leading the horses behind us.

Ava and Sarah were talking idly about the court when a voice called to Ava from across the street. I turned around and sucked in a sharp breath. It was Anhalt, one arm raised in greeting and a broad smile on his face.

I had just enough time to whisper his name to Ava and Sarah before he had crossed over to join us. I was careful to keep my face free of all emotion as Sarah and I dropped back to walk respectfully behind Ava and the count.

Anhalt seemed delighted with our chance encounter and determined to make the most of his unexpected audience with the queen. I watched the surrounding streets with my usual vigilance while I wondered if his voice really sounded so oily, or if it was my own feelings painting my perception of them.

Sarah was listening intently to their conversation, her eyes never leaving the count's form. I knew she would be paying attention for any clues, so I stopped listening myself, devoting my full attention to watching for any threat to the queen.

I wasn't sure if it was this extra attentiveness or just a heightened sense of alert due to the count's presence, but I noticed an odd flicker of movement as we passed a small side alley. It was barely more than a shifting of shadow, and I could easily have missed it. Instead I tensed, my hand flying to my sword hilt.

In one step, I placed myself between Ava and the alley. She turned to look at me, surprised out of her conversation by my sudden movement. I spoke to her but kept my eyes trained on the shadows.

"It might be nothing, but I think it would be a good idea if we moved a bit faster, Your Majesty."

Sarah let out a quickly stifled squeak, but Ava said nothing, merely lengthening her stride. I moved my gaze away from the potential threat to scan the area around us. We were in a fairly quiet side street, and there was still some distance to go before we reached the next crossroads.

If there was a threat, we weren't going to make it there in time. I chewed on the end of my tongue in concentration, frantically trying to formulate a plan. Coming up ahead of us, on the opposite side of the street to the alley, was a large shopfront. It was closed, the windows shuttered, but the entryway to the store was set back from the street front, down two steps.

"Over there, that doorway," I gestured toward the shop as I muttered the words to the other three. "Get down there, quickly."

Ava only had time for a single step in the direction of the meagre shelter when three armed men charged from the shadows of the side street.

"Hurry!" I yelled and heard Ava drop her horses' bridle and begin to run.

Our increased pace had taken us far enough from the alley entrance that the queen was able to reach the minimal safety of the doorway before our attackers reached us. I drew my own sword as I stepped backwards, placing myself in front of the two stairs.

I risked a single glance behind me to assure myself that Ava was in position and noticed that Anhalt was lingering at the top of the stairs, his hand on the hilt of his own sword.

"Get down there," I said, sweeping my arm backwards to indicate he should join Ava. My duty was clear. If at all possible, I needed to protect the nobleman as well as the queen.

But I was glad to see he was wearing a blade. If any of the attackers made it past me, he would be Ava's last line of defense. He didn't respond immediately, but when Ava snapped a command I heard his footsteps moving toward her.

I had assumed that Sarah would join the others but instead sensed her at my side. As the men closed on us, I angled myself to shield her with my body. Out of the corner of my eye I saw a long knife in her hand. She trembled visibly, but her expression was determined. I felt a swell of pride and fear, and then the men were upon us.

They attempted to rush us all at once, but our position and the milling horses made it difficult. One fell back and the other two attacked, swords raised. Sarah's knife would provide little defense against them.

I parried the first thrust and desperately tried a simple trick, twisting my blade to disarm my opponent. Even a moderately skilled swordsman could guard against it, but to my surprise, my attacker's blade went flying across the street.

I instantly ignored the man, side stepping and whipping my sword back to parry the second attacker. The first man was only disarmed, but I was hoping he would take the time to retrieve his sword.

The second man managed to evade my first two attacks while the third man stepped forward, eyes trained on me.

I lunged desperately, using all my strength to beat back my current attacker. To my relief, he was too slow to block me. My sword slid cleanly into his shoulder. He cursed loudly, dropping his weapon to the ground with a clang.

I shifted my weight to my back foot and kicked him hard in the stomach. He staggered backwards and fell to the street.

In the space of one panting breath, the third man had taken his place. More determined than the other two, he was quick to attack. He drove me back several steps. A half cry from Ava alerted me just as the back of my foot felt the edge of the top step.

I leaned dangerously backwards to avoid his next thrust and then drove forward with an attack of my own. My sudden ferocity surprised him, and he fell back into the middle of the street. I feinted toward his shoulder, where I had hit the other man, and he reacted with a desperate block. I used his distraction to step forward and sweep my leg across his feet.

He cried out and fell heavily to the ground. His hands flew out instinctively to catch himself, and he lost his grip on his sword. I knelt down and smashed him across the head with the hilt of my own weapon. His eyes rolled up, and he lost consciousness.

For a second I knelt there beside him, gulping for air and steadying myself. Then I remembered the first man. He had never renewed his attack against me and by stepping into the street, I had left the path to Ava open.

I leaped to my feet and spun around, fear filling my mind.

SARAH

I don't like knives. I avoid fights. I *hate* blood.

But I also know my duty, and I couldn't leave Evelyn to face our attackers alone. Ava must have read the determination in my face because she leaned out of the doorway to pass me a knife. A quick look passed between us, and I knew that it was killing her to huddle in the doorway and let us protect her. But she knew her duty, too.

I tried to stop my hand from shaking and guiltily felt relieved when Evelyn angled herself in front of me.

The first attack came so quickly that I could hardly follow it. I felt sure I was about to be cut down when suddenly my attacker was disarmed. Evelyn stepped away to deal with the other assailants, but I stayed frozen in place, my terrified gaze fixed on the now unarmed man in front of me. I wondered if I should step forward and attack him, but my feet stayed firmly in place.

He glanced at his sword, lying some way down the street and then at the queen and count behind me. Finally, he transferred his gaze to my shaking hand.

He obviously decided I wasn't much of a threat because he abandoned his sword, instead charging unarmed toward the narrow doorway. For half a second I stood frozen. And then my body responded automatically. I took one step forward and thrust my knife straight ahead of me.

The blade buried itself in his stomach with a sickening sound and an even worse sensation. I let go of the hilt and stepped backwards, my eyes wide and my whole body trembling.

The man looked down at my knife and then up at me in surprise. He reached forward as if to grab me but instead collapsed onto his knees and then down onto his side.

Blood began to pool around him, and I felt myself start to go faint. I swayed once and then steadying hands gripped me from behind. I recognized them as Ava's. I took two deep breaths and the blackness receded.

I turned toward her gratefully, but my eyes once again passed over the injured man on the ground. My stomach heaved uncontrollably and when Evelyn returned from dispatching the final man, instead of proudly standing guard over Ava, I was vomiting into the gutter.

Not my finest hour.

Still, the praises Evelyn and Ava heaped on me were almost enough to make me forget the groans of the man I had injured. Anhalt remained silent, his expression rather sullen, and the other two seemed to have almost forgotten him.

I hadn't, however, and I kept a sharp eye on him.

I was hoping we would move away from the location of the fight since the smell of blood kept making my stomach heave. Evelyn, however, was reluctant to leave the small amount of shelter offered by the shop doorway. Instead she whistled loudly in a complicated pattern, and I was just able to hear an answering whistle from beyond the crossroads.

"Good," said Evelyn. "There's a watchman nearby. He'll pass the call along to the closest squad of soldiers."

She kept us all in position for several tense minutes before I heard the distant tramp of feet. Sure enough, a small squad of soldiers appeared, heading toward us at full trot. When their leader caught sight of Evelyn, he barked an order and they picked up their pace.

Evelyn gestured for Ava to emerge from the doorway, and the soldiers quickly formed a protective barrier around her. Anhalt and I were included in the bubble of protection, but Evelyn remained outside. After a brief exchange of words with the leader of the squad, we set off back to the castle.

One runner was sent ahead, and two soldiers stayed behind to guard the wounded men. I didn't envy them the job and, from their expressions, they didn't much appreciate it, either. They kept looking nervously around, as if expecting to be assaulted by the men's friends at any moment. I assumed the runner had gone for more help and hoped, for the sake of the remaining guards, that he would be quick.

As we approached the castle, two groups came speeding from the front gates. One group passed us with nothing but a quick salute, but the others formed a second barrier of bodies around our existing guards and swept us into the safety of the castle walls.

Hans came rushing from the door of the castle, and the guards melted before him. In two large strides, he had Ava in his arms and was murmuring something into her hair. She was shaking her head against his chest, and I assumed she was reassuring him that she was unhurt.

I thought, a little wistfully, about how nice it would be to have someone rushing out of the castle to check on my safety. An image of Miles flashed through my mind, but I shook my head. It was no use thinking such thoughts.

As the rest of the guard dispersed, sent to man a double watch at the gates and along the wall, I saw another figure come striding around the edge of the castle. After a moment, I recognized him as Jake and was pleased to note that his face reflected some of the worry I had seen in Hans. I watched his eyes search the crowded courtyard and then settle on Evelyn. His gaze raked her up and down, and he visibly relaxed when he saw she was uninjured.

I smiled to myself. *That*, at least, was going well.

Evelyn hadn't seen him, but I was still watching him closely when I saw his steps falter. I followed the new direction of his eyes and saw they had moved to Anhalt. The count had also seen Jake, and I struggled to determine whose face held more animosity.

Well, well, well, I thought. *Clearly those two are not allies.*

I waited with great interest to see what would happen next, but Anhalt muttered a farewell and strode off into the castle. I was glad to see him go but a little disappointed to have missed a promising confrontation. It would have been quite exciting and just the thing to drive the lingering scent of blood from my mind.

While I had been distracted, Evelyn and Hans had decided to move us all into the castle. I looked over my shoulder as I mounted the steps into the entryway and saw Jake standing alone in the courtyard, his gaze fixed on our retreating figures. I didn't think that Evelyn had even seen him, and I felt another rush of disappointment.

I would tell her about it, of course, but I wasn't sure if she would believe me.

We were all ushered into Ava's council room and took seats around the polished table. I was only listening with half an ear as Ava and Evelyn recounted our adventure to Hans, Adelmar and the captain of the guard. The other two men had appeared in the room only seconds after we did, and I suspected that news of the attack was rapidly spreading throughout the castle.

I used the time to consider the details of everything that had happened and everything I had seen. Something didn't feel quite right, and I wanted to get my thoughts straight before I said anything to the others.

"There were only three?" Something in Hans' voice suggested

he was surprised by the number. I returned my full attention to the conversation.

"Yes," said Evelyn, and her voice reflected his confusion. "There's no question there was something strange about the whole thing. It was hardly the sort of polished attack I would have expected against a reigning monarch. The men weren't even very skilled." She paused thoughtfully and then hurried to add, "Not that I'm complaining."

"I think I might know why that was," I said, looking around the table in anticipation of seeing the same understanding in the faces of the others. Instead I got blank looks.

"Really?" I opened my eyes as wide as they would go and looked around again.

"Come on, Sarah, out with it." Evelyn rolled her eyes.

I opened my mouth to give a dignified reply but was interrupted by the door opening. A guard came in and leaned down to whisper something in the captain's ear. The older man nodded acknowledgment before dismissing the messenger.

When the door had closed, he directed a thoughtful look around the table.

"I find myself even more interested than ever to hear the young lady's theory. Something about this situation definitely doesn't add up. The three attackers are still being treated by some of the guard's doctors, and we naturally haven't had a chance to conduct an interrogation. However, one of my men has recognized them. They're mercenaries from one of the outer regions. Recently arrived in Rangmeros and mostly to be found at one of the seedier taverns. They're not too skilled apparently but also not too scrupulous about what sort of job they'll accept. I suspect we'll have no great trouble getting them to talk. Unfortunately, I'm equally confident they'll tell us they have no idea who hired them, they'll just know the man had gold."

He rubbed his face and sighed. "So, I'm hoping you do have

some insight for us, miss. It would certainly make my job from here a lot easier."

I shrugged. "I don't know how much assistance it will be in the investigation. It's only a theory, after all, I don't have any proof."

"Get on with it," said Evelyn.

I shot her an offended look but decided against replying. I didn't want to push her too far.

"I note that one member of our adventure is conspicuous only by his absence," I said, instead.

"Anhalt," said Evelyn.

"Exactly." I exchanged a significant look with her.

"I thought he wanted to influence Ava not assassinate her," said Hans, the skepticism clear in his tone and expression.

"You've all commented that the attempt was surprisingly insufficient." I shrugged my shoulders. "I don't think it was ever meant to succeed at all. I was watching Anhalt pretty closely, and his reactions seemed off. He didn't look surprised when we were attacked, and some of the looks he gave Evelyn were positively murderous.

"But he looked most annoyed when Ava ordered him to take cover. I suspect he orchestrated the attack with the intention of playing the hero and rescuing us all. If Evelyn had been less competent, and if she'd never overheard his conversation with the other nobles, it might have worked, too."

Evelyn looked outraged, presumably at the suggestion that Anhalt had gambled on her inability to do her job, but Hans looked a little relieved. I could imagine how pleased he must feel to know there wasn't an assassin waiting out there, ready to try again.

No one contradicted my conclusion although the captain looked disappointed.

"You're certainly right on one point," he said. "I can't go making any arrests based on that information. I'll start inquiries, of course, but if it was Anhalt, he'll have covered his tracks, I'm sure. And I'd need much more certain information than a guess before I could bring a noble in for questioning."

I nodded, disappointed but not surprised. As I did, my eyes happened to catch Adelmar's across the table. He looked neither angry nor surprised. Instead his frown showed cold calculation. I smiled. If the captain of the guard couldn't do anything about Anhalt, maybe Miles' father could.

EVELYN

$\mathcal{I}$t was an insult, of course. Three poorly trained ruffians and Anhalt was expecting to play the hero? How many other people in Rangmere thought me so incompetent?

As a female guard, I was used to being underestimated—I'd used it to my advantage plenty of times. In this role, it was less of an advantage though. I was representing not only myself but also the crown. If Ava's personal guard looked weak, so did she. It might encourage her enemies to attack.

Should I resign? The question rolled around and around in my head the next day until I decided to go to the training yard and burn off some energy. Hans had pressed Ava to take another day off after the scare, and I wasn't appreciating all the free time.

This time when I arrived, a group of guards were already involved in a series of training exercises. I recognized many of them from my practice session two days ago. I took a spot across the yard from them and began my warm ups.

While I stretched, I watched them. They spanned a range of ages and seemed, for the most part, fairly competent. Plenty of glances were thrown my way, some more open than others, and I was surprised how few of them were obviously hostile.

Perhaps word of the fight the day before had increased the guards' respect for me. It would be a very nice side effect of the otherwise unpleasant encounter.

Just as I was regaining my confidence, I met the eyes of the guard who I had beaten two days ago. The level of hatred on his face almost made me flinch. I forced myself to hold his gaze, however, and after a moment he looked away. He muttered something to the guard next to him, the man who had attempted to trip me, and they both moved to the other end of the training yard.

I sighed.

"That's a heavy sigh for a guard who just saved the queen's life," said a cheerful voice behind me.

I recognized it instantly but didn't turn around. I wanted the extra seconds to regain my composure. Sarah had told me about the animosity between Jake and Anhalt, but I still wasn't completely sure what I thought about him. I wanted to trust him too much. And I didn't like it when my emotions got involved with my judgment.

"Morning," I said, still facing forward.

He strode into view and leaned against one of the fence posts beside me.

"Still as humble as ever, I see." He gave me the easy grin I'd already started to see in my dreams, and I quickly looked away.

I let my eyes linger on the other guards and, after a moment, his own gaze followed mine.

"Everyone's talking about it, you know," he said. "A lot of the guards are really impressed."

I shrugged. "Not all of them."

Jake's eyes searched the group until they found the same two guards I'd been watching earlier.

"Well, you can never please everyone." His voice was light, but

I noticed a slight crease between his eyes. I wondered what the men had been saying about me.

"Why are you out here?" I asked after a moment of silence.

Jake looked at me with raised eyebrows, and I flushed slightly.

"Training with the guards, I mean," I said. "Why don't you spend your time with the other nobles?"

An expression of distaste crossed Jake's face before it smoothed back out to its usual good humor.

"I'm the lowest of the low when it comes to the nobles," he said. "I barely count at all. And I don't like court games. When it comes to intrigue, I've been outmaneuvered before. I prefer to fight my battles with a sword."

I waited for him to elaborate, but he didn't say any more. I repressed a sigh. Just what I needed—more mystery surrounding Jake.

I finished my stretches and shook out my limbs. Jake wasn't in training clothes, so I couldn't ask him for another practice bout. I glanced uneasily across at the other guards.

To my surprise, one of them had noticed that I was finished and was making his way toward me. He looked young but was very tall and moved with the easy confidence of a born fighter.

"Morning, sir," he said, giving Jake a mock salute and a smile.

Jake grinned back at him. "Evelyn, meet Turner, Turner, Evelyn."

I nodded at the newcomer. "Pleased to meet you."

"I thought I'd come over and congratulate you," he said. "I hear you took out three soldiers who had their eyes on our queen."

"Ruffians more than soldiers," I said.

"Ha! See, I told you she was modest." Jake was still grinning at Turner, and I was suddenly dying to know what else he'd said about me. I pushed the thought away.

"You're right, as always." Turner seemed almost as cheerful as Jake. They made a good pair.

"The truth is, I was hoping you might be interested in a practice bout. I wasn't here the other day, and I missed seeing you in action."

I weighed him up for a moment and then nodded. "Why not?"

As we prepared for the fight, several more guards drifted over and began to form a loose circle around us. A few of them called out encouragements to Turner, but none of them seemed hostile toward me. Some of the hope from earlier returned.

It didn't take long for me to work out that Turner's skill level fell somewhere between that of Jake and the other guard. In fact, his fighting style felt familiar enough that I suspected he often trained with Jake.

We fought for ten long minutes before he managed to land a winning blow.

"Good fight," he said, as we shook hands. "It could easily have gone the other way." I was gratified to see nods of agreement from all around. "Best of three?"

"No you don't, Turner," called out one of the other guards.

"Yeah, we want a chance," chimed in another.

I was soon besieged with requests for practice bouts and Turner fell back, laughing, before his comrades. I fought four more of them and managed to win all four matches. From the banter around me, it was soon obvious that Turner was well-liked and well-respected. A thought grew in my mind.

When I called a halt, there were cries of disappointment, but I stood firm. Eventually the other guards disbanded, and I was once again alone with Jake. We wandered back toward the castle, and I hated just how much I enjoyed his solid, cheerful presence by my side. I wanted to ask him straight out about Anhalt, but I didn't dare.

"You fought well," he said, at last, breaking the silence between us.

Despite my misgivings, I felt a warm glow at his words.

"I'm glad you weren't hurt yesterday." His second comment

was much quieter and made me glance over at him. His eyes, filled with concern, were fixed on me. "When I heard you were attacked while alone with Count Anhalt and Queen Ava, I was worried for you."

I examined his expression, trying to decide if there was something strange about his wording, or if it was just my paranoia. What exactly was there between Jake and the count?

I had just decided to ask him straight out when a voice called to him from behind us. When he saw who it was, he made his apologies and bid me farewell.

"My steward," he said ruefully. "I'm afraid I've been avoiding him all morning."

I bid him a polite farewell and continued into the castle alone. The unanswered questions swirled in my mind. I attempted to shrug them off and direct my thoughts down a different path. I hadn't gotten any answers from Jake but on another matter...

I directed my steps toward the captain of the guard's office.

His head was deep in paperwork when I entered, and he looked relieved to be interrupted. When I explained my purpose, he leaned back in his chair and regarded me thoughtfully.

"Aye," he said, after several long seconds. "His Majesty mentioned to me that they were wanting a second personal guard for the queen. Unfortunately, the matter has been overshadowed by the events of yesterday."

He was silent again, and I had to repress the urge to shift restlessly on my feet.

"I'm curious as to why you've brought this name to me? You could have made your suggestion directly to Her Majesty. She clearly has a soft spot for you, so I'm sure she would have accepted it readily enough."

I considered my words carefully.

"You are the captain of the guard and my superior officer. It's appropriate that any recommendation for the position should come through you. I can only give a suggestion based on a single day's observation, and I wouldn't trust the queen's life to one day's observation. You're the one who really knows the guards under your command."

I held my breath, hoping my response had satisfied him.

After another long examination, he nodded his head.

"That is correct," he said. "Your observations are noted. I'll move Turner to the top of the list of candidates under my consideration."

I gave him my thanks and made my escape. Today had gone well, but it didn't change the fact that I was proving to be a liability to my friend. I didn't want to leave Ava in the lurch, though. I figured I would wait until the captain of the guard had chosen another personal guard before I handed in my resignation.

SARAH

$\mathcal{I}$ sat in one of the smaller courtyards of the castle and stared at the bubbling fountain in front of me. There was no one else in sight, so I pulled my feet up onto the bench and hugged my knees.

Yesterday I had defended my own life and that of my friends, and I was quite proud of myself. But, I couldn't seem to stop reliving the feeling of my knife plunging into the attacker's body. The awful sound it had made kept playing over and over again in my head, and I was concentrating on not being sick.

Evelyn had taken down the two other men, and yet earlier today I'd seen her heading out to the training yard, as calm as ever. I wished I could be so brave.

Once again, the sickening sound ran through my head. I shivered and closed my eyes.

"There you are!"

I didn't move in response to the familiar voice, I was too busy keeping down the contents of my stomach.

"Sarah?" The tone changed to one of concern and someone sat down on the bench beside me. A warm hand began to rub my back.

I concentrated on the calming sensation and let the other thoughts flow away. Gradually I began to feel better. When I finally returned to something approaching normal, I opened my eyes.

Miles was looking at me with an expression of concern. I drew a deep breath and produced a smile.

"I'm sorry," I said.

"Don't be." His reply came quickly. "Is it about yesterday? My father told me what happened. I can't believe you were attacked like that!" His eyes drifted away from me and became hard and angry. One of his hands curled into a fist.

"Well, they weren't exactly attacking me."

"No, of course not." He looked only slightly appeased. "But you shouldn't have been left so vulnerable. You haven't had any training like your cousin."

I sighed. "The truth, of course, is that none of us should have been so vulnerable. I imagine Hans is currently in the process of convincing Ava that she should never leave the castle without a large escort of guards."

I chewed on my lip thoughtfully. "I wonder if she'll listen to him."

Miles reached out and took my hand. His clasp felt strong and warm and strangely intimate. I stared at our entwined hands.

"Well, I hope you'll listen to me," he said, his eyes intent on my face, "and not put yourself in such a dangerous position again."

I stared, mesmerized, into his warm brown eyes. He was concerned for me. He truly cared what happened to me. It was a heady thought.

I let myself revel in it for a moment before pulling myself back down to earth. I gently extricated my hand and returned my gaze to the fountain.

"I definitely think that would be for the best," I said, nodding. In fact, I wholeheartedly agreed with him and would be lending my support to Hans' plans for an armed escort.

I glanced back at Miles and saw that he was watching me with a slightly disappointed expression. He opened his mouth to say something, and I quickly cut him off.

"You left the ball in rather a hurry the other night. How did your chat with your father go?"

He snapped his mouth closed, his brain clearly scrambling to catch up with the change of topic. After a moment, he laughed a little guiltily.

"Was I that transparent?"

I laughed, too. "As clear as glass."

"I just get so frustrated." He slammed one of his fists into his leg. "He complains that I don't take my family responsibilities seriously enough, but then he goes and treats me like a child. How can I learn how to take on a serious role at court, if he doesn't even bother to keep me informed?"

I opened my mouth and then shut it again, deciding his question was rhetorical. Sure enough, he went on, not appearing to notice my lack of reply.

"I know he's planning some sort of countermove against Anhalt, and I want to be part of it. Or at least part of the planning." He blew out a frustrated breath. "He tells me I need to live up to our family name, and I think I could if he would give me a chance. It seems pretty clear he doesn't think I can contribute anything to his strategies."

I could actually hear his teeth grinding together.

"And now he's been called back to our family estates over some urgent matter. Personally, I think the timing seems highly suspicious, but he wasn't interested in my opinion. He says he has complete trust in his steward and that the man wouldn't have called him back unless it was truly important."

He sighed and shook his head.

Gingerly I reached out and placed my hand over his clenched fist.

He looked down at it in surprise and then took a deep breath, slowly relaxing his muscles.

"Does he have the same expectations of Annabelle?" I asked, struggling to imagine his shy younger sister getting involved in court machinations.

"Oh, no." He shook his head emphatically. "Annabelle is the sweetest girl in the Four Kingdoms, but she would hate a life at court. Even Father has accepted that. She only came down for the coronation."

His eyes seemed to focus on me properly for the first time since we had begun talking of his father.

"My apologies," he said, with a smile. "None of this is your fault. I shouldn't be unloading on you like this."

"No, don't be silly." I shook my head. "You can say anything you like to me. Part of being a merchant is knowing how to listen and how to keep your mouth shut afterwards."

He threw me a curious look.

I grinned. "You'd be surprised how many people will talk themselves into a sale when presented with a listening ear."

He smiled back at me and twisted his hand under mine, capturing my fingers before I could withdraw them.

"Sarah," he said, his voice serious and his gaze once again focused on my face.

My heart leaped and then began to race. I couldn't seem to get a full breath.

"Ahem." The moment was broken by a loud throat clearing behind us.

Miles looked almost savage as he wheeled around to face the intruder, but his expression changed to one of surprise when he saw who it was.

The man looked vaguely familiar, but it took me several seconds to place him. Adelmar's body servant. I wondered why he hadn't accompanied the lord on his unexpected return home.

He held out a sealed piece of parchment to Miles who took it, still looking bemused.

"This is addressed to my father." Miles' voice was sharp.

"Yes, my lord." The servant's face and voice were equally impassive. "Lord Adelmar left instructions that his communications should be delivered to you in his absence."

I beamed at Miles, delighted at this evidence of his father's trust.

Miles still looked more confused than happy, but he accepted the missive.

"Who is it from?" he asked.

I wondered if he was reluctant to open it.

"That, I couldn't say, sir." The servant hesitated for a moment as if debating whether to continue. "It was discovered on Lady Annabelle's pillow. I believe we weren't meant to find it until the morning as her ladyship retired earlier this afternoon and left instructions that she was not to be disturbed for the rest of the evening. However, Lord Adelmar left very specific orders regarding his daughter's care. Her maid has just discovered the room empty and this communication in her place."

Nothing about the servant's demeanor suggested that he had any particular opinions about the information he was imparting. I looked uneasily between the man and Miles. It almost sounded as if…

"Are you suggesting that my sister has run away?" Miles sounded outraged.

"Certainly not, my lord."

"I should hope not. You've known Annabelle her whole life and know that she would never dream of doing such a thing."

"As you say, my lord."

I couldn't help but wonder what the servant was really thinking under his professional detachment.

"Thank you, you can go."

The servant left without attempting any further communication, and Miles stared at the sealed parchment in his hand.

"I don't like this," he muttered.

"No, of course not. The whole thing seems very odd indeed. But you won't learn anything more by staring at it."

Miles seemed startled by my words, and I wondered if he'd forgotten my presence. I was aware that the letter might contain something personal, but I didn't offer to leave. I was far too curious for that.

Nodding his head, Miles ripped open the seal and scanned the contents. His face paled.

"What is it?" My voice came out sharper than I'd intended.

"Someone has abducted my sister." I thought I had seen Miles look angry before, but it was nothing to how he looked now.

"What do you mean?" I was struggling to accept his words. They seemed too fantastic.

"I mean that someone has taken my sister and means to hold her to ransom." His words were as hard and cold as the seat I was sitting on.

"But...who? Do they sign it?" I tried to peer over his shoulder at the words.

"Of course not, but there can't be any doubt, can there?"

"Anhalt." I had to agree with him—the count seemed the only likely option.

"He's miscalculated though." Miles leaped to his feet and a feral smile spread across his face. "The servants weren't supposed to find this until tomorrow and then they were supposed to send it on to my father at our estates. They must think they have a big head start. They may even still be in the castle."

He strode quickly out of the courtyard, and I rushed to follow him. I wasn't quite as sure as he seemed about the likelihood, or wisdom, of trying to locate the kidnappers within the castle.

"We need to report this to Ava and Hans," I said, having to take two steps for every one of his.

"There's no time." Miles didn't break his determined pace.

I grabbed his arm and pulled him to a stop.

"Where are you even going?" I let my exasperation show in my voice.

"To Anhalt's rooms. He has a large suite with easy access to one of the side courtyards and smaller gates. He's probably planning to smuggle Annabelle out as soon as it gets dark."

He pulled his arm out of my grip and turned to continue walking before suddenly pausing. He looked back at me, and I hoped he was starting to see sense.

"You're right, though," he said.

I breathed a sigh of relief.

"Confronting Anhalt could be dangerous. You shouldn't come with me."

"Miles!" This was not what I had intended.

"Yes," he seemed increasingly pleased with the idea. "It's far better if you don't come. I don't want to lose any time but we might need back up. You should go and inform the queen what has happened. Ask for a squad of soldiers to be sent to Anhalt's rooms."

I hesitated, hating to let him go on alone but also seeing the necessity of informing Ava what was happening. He used my hesitation to break away and start back down the corridor.

"Hurry," he said over his shoulder, and after one last concerned look at his retreating back, I set off running toward the royal suites.

EVELYN

J exited my room and wandered toward Sarah's suite. She had been looking unusually pale ever since the fight yesterday, and I decided to join her for dinner. Brooding wouldn't do her any good.

Of course, I was struggling to follow my own advice. All afternoon my mind had returned to the question of Jake. My heart wanted to trust him, but my head wasn't ready to give up the fight.

Despite my distraction, I was still instantly aware of the sound of running feet. I turned, curious to see who was in such a hurry. It was Sarah. It took her several moments longer to recognize me, and when she did she tried to stop but only succeeded in running into me.

"Oof." I grabbed her arms and just managed to keep us both on our feet. "What in the kingdoms are you doing?"

"Evelyn, oh thank goodness." She paused for a moment to regain her breath. "It's Miles! Or rather, it's Annabelle. I need to speak to Ava."

I was used to Sarah's dramatic ways, but something in her tone told me this was serious.

"She isn't in her suite. She and Hans have gone for a quiet meal somewhere. One of the smaller dining rooms, I suppose. I'm not sure which one."

"Oh dear." Sarah wrung her hands together, looking as if she was about to be sick.

My concern increased.

"I'm sure we can find her. What's happened?"

"It's Anhalt," she said. "Or at least, we think it is. Adelmar's been called back to his estates, and someone has kidnapped Annabelle."

"Kidnapped Annabelle?" I stared at her. "When?"

"Sometime earlier this afternoon. They left a note in her room."

"Impossible!"

Sarah shook her head, a distracted expression on her face. "It's not at all impossible, I assure you. I saw the message myself."

"And I saw Annabelle. Not half an hour ago. She was walking down the corridor with those other two attendants from the wedding. She looked perfectly calm, too."

"But, but…I don't understand. Are you completely sure?"

"Of course I'm sure!" I crossed my arms.

Sarah gasped and grabbed my arm.

"Miles!" Her eyes were wide. "It must be a trap. It's the only thing that makes sense. Anhalt must have been hoping that Miles would do exactly what he's done and head straight to Anhalt's rooms to confront him."

I was a little less sure of her conclusion. "It hardly seems like a sure plan. What if Miles had gone to Ava instead?"

"The message wasn't signed. He could have simply denied any involvement. But he must have known that Miles would react that way if his sister was threatened." She was already pulling me back down the corridor. "If we hurry, we might be able to catch him before he gets there."

That, at least, sounded like a sensible plan. I shook off Sarah's hand and began to run in earnest. Sarah was soon trailing several steps behind me, her breathing labored.

When I turned into Anhalt's corridor without any sign of Miles, I stopped. Sarah once again crashed into me; this time into my back.

"Oh no." She moaned. "We're too late."

I looked at the closed door warily. "Are you sure he's in there?"

"Yes, yes, he must be. He was coming straight here when he left me."

"We need to find Ava, then," I said. "Only she has the authority to demand an immediate search of Anhalt's rooms."

I turned to retrace our steps, but Sarah started down the corridor toward Anhalt's door instead. I hurried after her.

When she reached it, she leaned forward and placed her ear against the wood. After a moment, she pulled back and shook her head.

"I can't hear any voices or movement," she whispered. "They might have already left." Her eyes flew to the external door located at the opposite end of the corridor from where we had entered.

Before I could protest, she had started for it. She had just touched the handle, presumably meaning to open it a crack and peer out, when the door was pulled open from the other side.

"Hey!" There was a startled exclamation from the soldier standing in the now open doorway.

Sarah gave a small scream and fell backwards, but the man reached forward and grabbed her by the arms. He looked almost as surprised as she did, his reaction clearly instinctive. Now that he had a firm grasp on her, however, he didn't look inclined to let go.

He called over his shoulder, presumably looking for instruction from whoever was in the courtyard, and I began to run toward them. Before I could reach the doorway, he yanked her forward, into the open air. I yelled and rushed out after them, wishing I was wearing my sword.

I only had a moment to take in the scene in the courtyard. There was no sign of the guard who should have been on the side gate, but the courtyard seemed full of soldiers. They looked like mercenaries.

The gate was open, and two of the men were about to leave the castle, dragging Miles between them. His head hung limply, and a trickle of blood ran down from a small cut above his eye.

Closer to me, two more soldiers were attempting to restrain a struggling Sarah. I started toward them but didn't make it more than two steps before at least five men charged toward me. I took out the first one with a solid punch to the jaw followed up by a knee in the groin. He fell to the ground groaning, but our brief fight had given the others time to draw their swords and surround me. Unarmed, I had no chance. I stilled.

"Ah, a sensible girl." The smooth voice of Anhalt made me grit my teeth. He emerged from the shadows and stood in front of me.

"I'm surprised you dare to show your face." I spat on the ground. "You must be mad to think you'll get away with this."

"You'd be surprised what I can get away with." The smile didn't leave his face, and I uneasily remembered Ava's talk of bewitchment. "And this is all your fault, really. I might not have had to resort to such drastic measures if you hadn't interfered yesterday.

"It's all turned out for the best, though. I never dreamed I'd get the two of you as well. With the queen's two closest friends gone and her Chief Advisor otherwise engaged, she'll truly have no one left to turn to."

I glared at him, all the time watching for any sign of weakness in the circle surrounding me and keeping half an eye on Sarah. While I had been talking with Anhalt, his men had bound and gagged her, but she looked unhurt.

If he intended to do the same to me, that would be my chance to fight. Unfortunately, he signaled one of the men to throw a length of rope at my feet instead.

"I'm afraid I'll have to trouble you to tie yourself up," he said, his tone of voice genial. "And I suggest that you don't try anything untoward. Not unless you want to see harm come to that lovely cousin of yours." His eyes flicked over toward Sarah, and I ground my teeth.

Sarah looked at me apologetically, and I knew that, if she could, she would have told me to ignore Anhalt and fight anyway. I would have done it, too, if I stood any chance at all. But there were simply too many of them.

I secured my hands as slowly as possible, hoping some castle guards might stumble into the courtyard. No one came.

I tried to tie the rope so that I could pull it loose later, but one of the watching soldiers cleared his throat loudly, and Anhalt shook his head at me.

"Now, now, Evelyn, no tricks, please." His eyes once again darted toward Sarah, and I sighed silently and tied the knots properly. The best I could do was leave myself a little bit of slack.

When I'd finished, Anhalt had me step through my own bound arms so that my hands were behind me. A sword tip at my back prodded me forward, and both Sarah and I were hustled out through the side gate.

Waiting on the other side was an open wagon. Rough hands lifted us into the back of it. A heavy tarpaulin was thrown over us, effectively cutting off any visibility and pinning us both flat against the floor of the wagon. I could hear the soldiers mounting horses and then the wagon jerked forward, causing me to slide into Sarah.

"Sorry," I whispered, but there was no response. I remembered that she was gagged.

Wriggling around, I managed to grab a handful of her clothing. It felt like a sleeve, but it wasn't the right material for Sarah's dress. I frowned and then realized it must be the semi-conscious Miles.

"Sarah?" I kept my voice low and hoped she could hear me.

It was hard to hear movement over the sound of the wheels on the road beneath us, but after a moment a foot kicked me in the shoulder.

"Ow!" I grumbled to myself as I carefully rolled over and slid forward until I could feel Sarah's shoulder. It was hard work with my hands behind my back, but I had managed to leave myself just enough slack that I was able to untie the gag from her mouth.

"Oh, thank goodness, that tasted horrible!"

I chuckled. Classic Sarah.

"Can you untie my hands?" She sounded hopeful.

"Sorry," I said. "I saw the knots they used, and there's no way I could get them undone with my hands tied like this. I have a knife in my boot, but it's too dangerous for me to get it out now. The way we're jolting around like this, I might accidentally slit one of our wrists instead of the rope."

I could almost hear Sarah wince.

"I think Miles is here with us." Just as I said it, there was a loud groan.

"Miles?" Sarah sounded worried.

There was a long pause and then a groggy, "Sarah?"

"Are you hurt? Do you have your hands free?" He'd been untied when I last saw him.

There was another long pause.

"My head's pounding, but the rest of me seems fine. They've tied my hands, though. I can barely move them."

I sighed. It had only been a slim chance.

"Someone must have cracked me over the head as soon as I got through the door," he continued. "It was like they were expecting me. Is Annabelle here, too?"

"What? Oh, right, you don't know." Sarah sighed.

"Don't know what?"

"Annabelle was never kidnapped," I told him. "I saw her myself back at the castle. She was with friends."

"I…I don't understand." I could hear the frown in Miles' voice.

"It was a trap," said Sarah. "It's the only explanation. It was you they were after."

"Me?" There was a thoughtful pause. "Then I guess it was a good thing I sent you for help. Otherwise no one would have any idea what's happened to us."

There was a pause. I assumed Sarah was as reluctant to disillusion him as I was.

"Yes, about that," she said at last, her voice guilty.

"Hey!" said Miles suddenly, cutting her off. "What are you even doing here? How did Anhalt get you, too?" His tone changed to one of foreboding. "You did go for help, right? Someone is coming after us?"

"Well, I did go for help, yes," said Sarah. "I found Evelyn." She paused again.

"And then…"

"And then Evelyn told me it must be a trap, and we tried to catch you before you walked into it."

There was yet another long pause and then a loud groan from Miles. "So, all three of us have walked into a trap, and no one else has any idea what's going on."

"That about sums it up, yes," I said, keeping my tone even.

SARAH

There was silence for a long time after my admission. I kept going over and over it in my mind, and wishing I had just left that courtyard door alone.

It wasn't making me feel very cheerful, but at least it was better than focusing on how much it hurt every time the wagon went over a bump. And there were a lot of bumps on this particular road.

I'll have to have a word with Ava about it when we get back, I thought. *She really should keep the roads in better condition.*

Somehow the thought made me feel instantly more optimistic. Of course, we would get back. And I would be far better off looking for opportunities to escape than moping.

I tried to guess where we were going. One of Anhalt's properties seemed like the most logical option, but I didn't know anything about his lands. I hoped wherever it was, it wasn't too far away. My hip was already one big bruise.

"Do either of you know where Anhalt's lands are?" It was Evelyn, voicing my own question.

"They're close," said Miles. "Maybe three hours west from the capital."

"That must be where we're going then," she said. "We came out the west gate."

"What do you think Anhalt plans to do with us?" I tried to keep the fear out of my voice.

"I'm sure he doesn't want to harm us." Miles was a little too quick with his response. Perhaps my fear had been evident after all.

"I think you're right," said Evelyn slowly. "He certainly seems to want Miles as some sort of bargaining chip against Adelmar. And he clearly planned the whole thing with great care. He won't want to throw away any advantage we might give him. Not until he's had a chance to think through all the different eventualities, anyway."

It made sense, and I should have thought of it myself.

"Anhalt must have been behind the message to Adelmar. It's just too convenient otherwise," I said.

"Yes, I've been thinking about that," said Miles. "And about the message that was delivered to me. Clearly my father's body servant must have been working with Anhalt, but it doesn't make any sense. Before this, I would have trusted my life to his loyalty without hesitation."

"Bewitchment," whispered Evelyn.

"What?" I asked, surprised that she of all people would leap to such a conclusion.

"Ava said there were rumors of Anhalt bewitching people. It might have been how he got his position in the first place. I don't suppose you have a godmother, Miles?" She tried to sound nonchalant, but I could hear the hope in her voice. Evelyn would hate the idea of fighting against something that couldn't be defeated with a sword.

"Unfortunately not," said Miles, his voice dry. "I'm neither a prince nor a deserving woodcutter's son. I'm not even a third son. Us noblemen have to muddle along on our own as best we can."

This wasn't very encouraging, and we all subsided back into silence again. I tried to calculate how long we'd been traveling and how much further we had to go.

After another long wait, the sound of the surface under the wagon wheels changed, and then we heard cries of greeting and the creaking of gates. We'd reached our destination.

"Sarah." Evelyn's whisper was urgent.

"Yes?"

"I've been thinking, and I'm pretty sure Anhalt is going to lock us up somewhere. Once the key turns, escape will get a lot harder. So, if you can, try to walk behind me. Get as close as possible without arousing any suspicion. If we get even a moment when we aren't surrounded and Anhalt's attention is distracted, go for the knife in my boot and use it to cut me free."

I hesitated for a fraction of a second before whispering my agreement. Sleight of hand was hardly one of my skills, and my heart rate was increasing just thinking about holding a knife again. I didn't see what choice I had, though.

When someone pulled off the tarpaulin, I was blinded by what seemed to be a blazing light. As someone pulled me roughly out of the wagon, my eyes gradually adjusted, and I was able to see that we were inside the courtyard of a small stone castle. A number of servants mingled with the soldiers, each holding a burning torch.

Evelyn and Miles were both in front of me and each were flanked by two rough looking men with drawn swords. Only one soldier was pulling me along by my arm, and his blade remained in his sheath. Clearly, I wasn't considered a threat.

I pretended to stumble so that I could move closer to Evelyn. My guard jerked at my arm but otherwise ignored my change in position. I reminded myself to breathe.

Anhalt directed his men with a constant stream of loud orders, and the courtyard soon began to empty. When only our guards remained, he directed us all through the castle courtyard.

It was hard to see much of the building in the dark, but it looked both older and considerably smaller than the royal castle at Rangmeros. The count's wealth was evident in the lavish interior decorations, and I resented him for having such good taste in furnishings. The stronghold of an evil count should be gloomy and unpleasant.

We were hustled through several corridors and down narrow, stone stairs. I began to suspect we were heading for a dungeon that would meet all my expectations for dank hideousness. I shivered.

When we reached the bottom of the second flight of stairs, we were greeted by a solid oak door. It had a large and ominous looking lock.

Anhalt turned and smiled at us. I looked away from his face in disgust, and my eyes fastened on a large, blood-red jewel that he wore around his neck on a thick gold chain. It shone brightly in the light of the torch Anhalt was holding, and I found it mesmerizing. It took me several long seconds to tear my gaze away from it.

"Ah," said Anhalt. He reached down to stroke the jewel, and I noticed that his eyes were resting on me. "I see that you've noticed my prize possession. An enchanting piece is it not?"

There was laughter in his voice, and I narrowed my eyes at him.

"But enough chit-chat." He rubbed his hands together. "One of my ancestors was a unique man, and he had an equally unique dungeon built. Apparently, he believed that prisoners were less likely to escape if they had something else to spend their energy on. I've never had the opportunity to use it myself, and I must say that I find the prospect rather entertaining."

He once again smirked at us all, but if he was hoping for a response he was disappointed.

"His strategy was to release all the prisoners to roam freely throughout the dungeon."

My spirits lifted at his words, and I was glad to know we would all be together. His next words were less heartening.

"I suppose in this case, you might find comfort in such a thing. Of course, you'll have to find each other first. And, personally, I'd recommend putting your energy into finding the slot where we'll be sliding through some food and water. It's not far from this entry." He chuckled. "But, of course, you'll have to find the entry first."

I now felt nothing but foreboding.

"Don't worry if you get lost, some guards will come by to find you...eventually. So, you might not want to burn too much of your energy." He chuckled again, and I wished I was strong enough to wring his neck.

Instead, while he was opening the door, I sidled closer to Evelyn's back. We were still accompanied by five guards, but I was hoping that Anhalt now felt secure enough that he wouldn't bring them all into the dungeon with us.

Sure enough, he dismissed three of them, and only six of us stepped into the stone corridor on the other side of the door. The meaning of his words was immediately obvious. We were surrounded on all sides by a giant, stone maze. How long would we spend stumbling around without food or water?

The two remaining guards seemed equally interested in the maze, and Evelyn used their distraction to signal me with her hands. We were all pressed closely together, and I doubted I could crouch down to her boot without being noticed. I finally admitted to myself that I didn't think I had the courage to try. I was frozen by fear. Just the thought of her knife brought the sickening sounds and sensations of my previous fight flooding back into my mind. I gritted my teeth, determined not to faint. I felt like crying at the thought of letting the others down.

Before any tears could fall, however, she spoke. Her words were so quiet I could barely hear them, and they were so unexpected, it took me a moment to understand her meaning.

"Quick, give me your necklace!"

Knowing I had only seconds before the guard's attention returned to us, I quickly bowed my head and slipped off the long, double strand of glass beads I was wearing. I placed them in her hands, and her fingers quickly closed over them.

"Well, come on then," said Anhalt sharply and one of the guards turned to prod Evelyn with his sword tip.

I stared at him closely, but he didn't seem to have noticed our exchange. As we walked along the corridor, I kept close behind Evelyn, hiding whatever she was doing with her hands.

When we reached the first turn, I felt rather than heard one of the beads drop to the dirt floor. I forced myself not to look down at it and inwardly praised Evelyn for her quick thinking. I still had no idea how we were going to escape but at least being able to find the door would be a start.

Anhalt led us through so many twists and turns that I soon grew hopelessly confused. It didn't help that the light was low and flickering and that every part of the maze looked the same.

"You know," said Anhalt, as if we were all in the middle of a friendly conversation, "I'm the only one who knows the way through the maze. But don't get any ideas, I'll be bringing plenty of guards with me when I come to find you. I imagine you might be feeling a little hungry by then. If you like, I'll ring a bell when I come through the door, and I recommend that you give me a shout to let me know where to start looking. Your choice, though." He shrugged. "I'll find you either way."

Once again, none of us responded.

"And here's our first stop." He turned and looked us all over. "I think we'll begin with you, merchant girl."

He was gesturing toward me, and I tried my best to look unaffected by my surroundings.

"You'll be staying here. And don't expect to see us coming back, we'll be leaving by a different route."

I didn't move so one of the guards reached forward and shoved me to the ground.

"Don't touch her," growled Miles, his eyes blazing at the guard.

His manner was so confident and assured that for a moment I forgot that he was the prisoner. I think the guard did, too, because he fell back a step, his expression uncomfortable.

"Very noble," said Anhalt dryly. "Now get moving."

The guard recovered and was quick to wave his blade in Miles' direction.

Miles threw me an apologetic and concerned look, and then the whole group began to move away down the corridor. Evelyn didn't even glance at me, and I knew she was trying not to attract any attention to herself. As they turned the corner and the light began to dwindle, I took heart from the sight of one of my beads falling quietly to the floor.

And then the light disappeared, and I wondered what use a trail of beads was going to be if we couldn't see it.

EVELYN

I silently cursed Anhalt for leaving Sarah sitting alone in the dark, but I carefully kept my face blank. The beads were our best chance, and I didn't dare draw any of the men's attention to me. My biggest concern was that Anhalt would leave me next. If that happened, I didn't know how we would find Miles.

I heaved an internal sigh of relief when we stopped for a second time and he instructed Miles to sit. Miles looked like he was about to rebel, so I risked meeting his eyes and giving my head the slightest shake.

Stay here, I mouthed as clearly as I could. I wasn't sure he'd understood me, but it was the best I could do.

When we began walking again, I was alone with Anhalt and the two guards. I suspected he was leaving us in reverse order of strength and would have been flattered if I wasn't so angry.

He was right, though. He didn't want me at his back, not when he only had two guards with him. He expected us to be weakened from hunger and thirst when he returned, but I suspected he would still bring a whole squad.

I intended for us to be long gone by then.

When I dropped my fourth-to-last bead, I began to feel a little nervous. How much further were we going to go?

We turned another corner. And then another. I rolled the last bead around and around in my hand and wondered if I could remember a few turns before I dropped it.

But then Anhalt stopped, and I almost smiled.

That was close.

He didn't stop to talk, merely instructing me to sit and then hurrying away with the guards behind him. He seemed nervous, and I suspected there was a door nearby where he intended to exit the maze. It was tempting to try to follow him, but I didn't dare risk it in the dark and with only one bead left.

Instead, I waited until the light had disappeared and then felt around in my boot for the hilt of my knife. My fingers clasped the blade awkwardly, struggling to saw through the ropes without cutting myself.

The knife slipped twice, but thankfully I received nothing worse than a graze. When the last fibers fell apart, I brought my hands in front of me and massaged my wrists. I winced as the blood flow painfully returned.

While I had been working, the seemingly impenetrable black of the maze began to slowly lighten. The change was almost imperceptible at first, and it took me several minutes to realize I was able to dimly make out the stones in the wall opposite me.

I looked around for the source and couldn't see anything. I shrugged. I didn't care if it came from a wishing star or a godmother's wand. I could see, and that was all that mattered.

I stood up and began to retrace my steps, eyes glued to the ground, searching for each of the beads. When I encountered one, I picked it up and slipped it into my pocket. My knife I left in my hand.

My eyes were aching from peering through the dim light when I picked up the bead that should have been around the corner from Miles. Unfortunately, when I turned into the next corridor, it was empty except for the scuff marks on the dirt floor where we had left him.

I exclaimed in annoyance. Clearly, he hadn't understood me.

I stood for a long moment, indecisive. I couldn't see any other option than to continue on to Sarah, however. Once we were together, we could consider how to find Miles.

As my pockets grew heavy and I counted only two more beads until I reached Sarah, I heard a low sound that could have been the murmur of voices. I paused and listened intently. The sound continued but there was no way to identify exactly what it was.

I continued on more cautiously. By the time I turned into Sarah's corridor, I was certain it was voices, and I was moving as silently as possible, my knife held ready at my side.

But it was a cry of welcome rather than alarm that greeted me as I moved into sight.

Sarah jumped to her feet and rushed over to hug me. I could just see her smile through the darkness.

"That was truly brilliant, Eve!" she said.

Miles was slower to get to his feet, but he also appeared to be smiling.

"What are you doing here?" I asked him. "I was worried when you weren't where we left you."

He held up one of Sarah's beads. "I was just wondering what I should do when I noticed someone had kindly marked the path. I could hardly sit around doing nothing after that."

I shook my head, but I was too relieved to feel annoyed with him for giving me a scare.

"Do either of you know where this light is coming from?" Sarah was looking around curiously, as mystified by the source of the glow as I was.

"It's moonlight," said Miles. "The underground levels of castles are always built with a series of thin shafts for ventilation.

It must be a bright night out there for so much light to be getting through."

I was glad to have the mystery solved. Sarah and I had no experience with castles, but it must have seemed like obvious knowledge to Miles.

We all began to walk back toward the entry, stepping carefully to avoid dislodging one of the beads in the now somewhat crowded corridor. I was considering what we would do when we reached the locked door, but Sarah's mind was obviously elsewhere. She interrupted my thoughts with an abrupt question.

"Did either of you notice that necklace Anhalt was wearing?"

"It was a little hard not to when he was stroking it like it was his first-born child," said Miles.

I had to chuckle at his apt imagery.

"When I looked at it, it was hard to tear my eyes away," said Sarah. "I think that's how he's enchanting people."

I considered the idea.

"It's possible, I suppose," I said. "There are certainly tales about charmed objects and so forth. It doesn't much matter one way or the other while we're trapped in here, though."

"No," said Miles, "but when we get out, we need to find a way to get our hands on that jewel. It might be our only hope of stopping Anhalt. Imagine if he managed to get close enough to the king and queen to use it on them?"

I shuddered. Now that was a terrifying thought. I began to move more quickly.

"Anhalt could be back in the capital tomorrow," I said, thinking aloud. "If he does plan to use it to influence Ava, now would be the perfect time. She's missing her personal guard, her only friends and her Chief Advisor. Who's going to stop him getting close to her?"

I wasn't sure how moving faster was going to help us when I hadn't worked out how to get through the door, but I couldn't help myself. We reached the door in what seemed like no time at all. I stared at it, disheartened. It was solid and thick and looked like it could withstand a battering ram.

"I don't suppose noblemen's sons are taught anything about picking locks?" I asked.

"Unfortunately not," said Miles. "It's increasingly clear that we're a rather useless lot."

I shot him an approving look, pleased that this ordeal hadn't destroyed his sense of humor. You never knew how nobles would take it when their pride was damaged.

Of course, all of us were feeling a little less amused an hour later when we still had no plan for getting through the door. I'd resigned myself to attempting to ambush Anhalt when he reappeared. I only hoped I wasn't too weakened by hunger, thirst and exhaustion when that moment came.

Sarah, as usual, maintained a more cheerful outlook than I did and had even managed to produce a small laugh at something Miles said to her when she suddenly stopped mid-chuckle and swung around to face the door. I had heard the same noise. It was unmistakably a key being put into the lock.

I signaled for Sarah and Miles to back up behind the door where they would be out of sight. There was no time for any further planning.

The door swung open, and I stepped forward, hoping to get the hilt of my knife against the skull of the newcomer before they saw me. If I was fortunate, I might have time to grab their sword before the next person realized what had happened.

I was swinging my arm around when I recognized the face in front of me. I fell back and let my arm drop to my side in shock.

The surprise was quickly replaced by bitter disappointment. My head had been right, after all. Jake was in league with Anhalt.

"Evelyn!" He seemed almost as astonished as I was. The expression was quickly replaced by his easy grin, however, and I felt a fresh surge of anger that he could smile at such a time.

"This is excellent. I was picturing myself spending days

searching through the maze for you, and I don't know if we have days."

I tried to make sense of his words through the haze of betrayal. Before I could think of anything to say, Sarah appeared from around the door, Miles close behind her.

"Sarah, Miles. Good, you're all here."

None of us returned his greeting, and his grin slowly faded at our accusatory expressions.

"What's wrong? Are you hurt?" He looked genuinely concerned and my confusion grew.

"What are you doing here, Jake?" I asked.

"Rescuing you, of course." He looked from face to face. "Oh, is that the problem? I'm not here with Anhalt, I came to set you free."

"And how do we know this isn't part of your cousin's grand plan?" asked Miles, his voice hard.

"Cousin?" Sarah sounded as stunned as I felt.

"Yes, didn't you know?" Miles glanced down at her. "Jake and Anhalt are first cousins."

"Why didn't you say anything?" I directed the question at Jake but felt like it applied equally to Miles.

Both men shrugged.

"Everyone knows it," said Miles.

"It's hardly something I'm proud of," said Jake at the same time.

The two noblemen weighed each other with their eyes.

"We might be family, but I bear no love for Anhalt. He's injured me more than anyone else," said Jake.

Miles nodded an acknowledgment of this point and exhaled. His tense shoulders relaxed in a clear gesture of belief.

"Jake's father was the last count," he explained to us. "Jake grew up expecting to one day take his father's place, but when he died, Anhalt came forward claiming the title was his. The magistrates upheld his claim, and the court hasn't quite known what to do with Jake ever since."

"I still had my knighthood, so they couldn't entirely throw me out," said Jake. "Many of them were suspicious of Anhalt's claim, but there was nothing they could do. I think seeing me makes them uncomfortable, it reminds them that no one is truly secure."

He paused to take a deep breath.

"I considered leaving, going to seek my fortune in Arcadia or Northhelm, but I couldn't allow Anhalt to enjoy my father's place. It's an insult to his memory. So, I've been waiting and watching, biding my time, gathering intelligence. At this point, I know that Anhalt has bewitched my people here in the castle, and I'm sure he used an enchantment on the magistrates, too. But I need to prove it."

"That jewel he wears around his neck," said Sarah, her voice rising with excitement. "I'm sure that's how he does it."

Jake nodded. "I agree. I got word yesterday morning that Anhalt had something big planned for today." He looked over at me. "That's why my steward interrupted us. I rode straight out here and have been lying in wait, hoping that Anhalt might finally misstep."

He shook his head.

"He's been very cautious until now, but he's definitely gone too far. With your testimony, the queen won't hesitate to have him arrested."

It was a shocking story, and yet it fit with everything we had already guessed. My uneasiness grew.

"Unless he gets to Ava before us and manages to use that jewel to bewitch her, too," I said.

Sarah's expression changed from excitement to horror, but Jake just nodded his head. He was already thinking the same thing.

"One of my father's old servants broke his leg," he said. "He was stuck in bed for two weeks, and he said that, after a few days, he felt like he was waking up from a dream. Anhalt's hold on him had broken. As soon as he could hobble around, he managed to sneak away and find me. According to him, it starts out like a gentle suggestion, and the more time the person spends around Anhalt, the stronger the compulsion to obey him becomes. So he won't be able to enchant the king or queen in the space of a moment. He'll need time. But a few days might be enough, which is why I was so glad to see you here at the door. How did you find your way back so quickly?"

I explained the trick with the beads, and he looked suitably impressed.

"You may well have saved the kingdom, Evelyn," he said, and I couldn't help but flush at the warmth in his voice. I just wished he had explained all of this to me before. I would have believed him. I think.

"How did you get the key?" asked Miles.

"I always had it," said Jake with a grin. "My cousin stole my title—I didn't exactly hand over my keys when I left."

"Talking about your cousin, do you have any idea where he is now?" I asked.

Jake frowned. "Unfortunately no. I focused all my attention on getting down here and rescuing you."

I knew he meant all of us when he said *you,* but somehow his statement felt personal and I flushed again. I shook my head. I needed to stay focused.

"Well, first things first, I want to find a proper weapon."

Miles echoed my sentiments, but I noticed that Sarah shrank back a little, her eyes fixed on the knife in my hand. This wasn't a good time for her to fall apart.

"Come on then," said Jake, "I'll take you to the armory." Neither of the men had noticed Sarah's hesitation, and after a moment she shook herself and followed behind us. I blew out a quiet breath of relief.

SARAH

*T*railed behind the others afraid of how I would respond to the sight of a room full of weapons. As it turned out, however, that would have been the lesser of two evils.

We were creeping through a room, several flights up from the dungeon, when a door suddenly opened, and a group of guards came in. The one in front was looking back over his shoulder, laughing with his comrades, so it took him a minute to see us. Unfortunately, even with that advantage, we were outnumbered and out armed.

Evelyn, as always, was in the lead. Before the man in front realized what had happened, she had knocked him to the ground and stabbed him in the shoulder. She drew his sword from his scabbard, but I couldn't drag my eyes away from the knife protruding from his body. My stomach heaved, and I scurried to the back of the room, cowering in a corner.

A scream from Evelyn pulled my eyes back to the fight. She was now holding the downed soldier's sword, but a second soldier had managed to stab her in the upper thigh. I opened my mouth to yell her name, but Jake got there first.

"Evelyn!" His voice was rough with fear, and he was running toward her, his own sword drawn. "Get back."

She beat off a second thrust from her attacker and managed to fall back behind Jake. Miles was close behind him, and he also called her name.

"Quick, give me the sword."

She hesitated for the briefest moment and then threw it to him. Moving slowly and wincing, she began to make her way back toward me.

Despite my concern over her injury, I was distracted by the sight of Miles going into battle. Now that I thought about it, I supposed all nobleman's sons received some training in combat, but he had never mentioned it, and I had never considered it before. For a second I felt afraid for him, and then my fears were forgotten.

He looked like he was on the dance floor instead of in the middle of a fight. His sword moved so quickly and with so much elegance that I almost forgot it was a weapon. I had seen Evelyn fight plenty of times before, but Jake and Miles fighting side by side had a different sort of elegance from her efficient moves.

The incoming soldiers were hampered by the width of the doorway, and Jake and Miles picked them off one by one, their blades flying beneath the soldier's guards with deceptive ease. Finally, there were no more opponents standing. I expected them to come back toward us at that point, but they both took off running down the corridor outside. I could only assume they were chasing someone who had gone to raise an alarm.

I suddenly remembered Evelyn was wounded and turned to her. She had reached me but was also staring after our departed allies.

"Well, thank goodness Miles can fight." Her voice sounded strained. It was hard to tell whether from the pain or from anger with herself for getting wounded in the first place.

I drew a deep breath and attempted to steel myself before looking at the wound on her leg. It was deep and the blood was gushing down over her knee. To my surprise, instead of feeling sick, I felt only fear for the blood she was losing.

"Sit down," I said, the worry making my voice sharp.

She obeyed, swaying as she did so, and I wondered if she had been about to fall. I flipped up my skirt and tore a long piece of material from the petticoat underneath. I folded it into a wad and pressed it against the wound.

"Hold this in place," I said.

As soon as she had a firm pressure on it, I bent down to tear off another piece. This one I used as a bandage, wrapping it several times around her leg. I knotted it as tightly as I could and stepped back.

Looking down at my hands I saw they were covered in blood. I waited for the nausea to surface, but I felt nothing except pride. My eyes welled with tears of gratitude. A wave of confidence washed over me. I wasn't weak. When it really mattered, I could do what needed to be done.

Evelyn was watching me, surprise in her eyes.

"Well done," she said. "And thank you."

I nodded at her, not quite trusting myself to speak.

I was still regaining my composure when Miles and Jake came racing back into the room. Jake didn't stop until he was kneeling beside Evelyn, carefully checking my bandage. Miles, however, hung back, his eyes darting between my hands and Evelyn's injury.

When his eyes settled on my face, they were full of pride. He understood my small victory, and the knowledge that he knew me so well nearly brought another rush of tears to my eyes. I shook them away.

"What now?" I asked, worried for Evelyn and worried that Anhalt might be escaping us.

"One of them tried to run for help, but we caught him." Miles' voice was grim.

"He was heading for the front entrance, though," said Jake. "It's possible my cousin hasn't left yet."

"We have to get going then." Evelyn attempted to pull herself to her feet but sank back with a groan.

"Useless," she muttered to herself.

Jake and Miles both came over and placed themselves on either side of her. Between the three of them, they got her to her feet. She insisted she was fine, although her face had lost all color, and we were able to move forward with her arms slung over the shoulders of the men.

I could tell that all four of us found the slow pace agonizing, but no one said anything. When we passed the soldier lying in the corridor, I averted my face but was pleased not to feel faint.

Several corridors later, Jake signaled that we should halt and pointed toward a door. "That's the entrance hall."

Sure enough, we could hear the sounds of feet and several raised voices coming from the other side. After my last experience with attempting to peek through a doorway, I had no desire to approach it.

Thankfully, Miles didn't feel any nervousness. He strode forward and eased the door open a crack. After a moment, he slid it closed again and returned to us.

"He's there," he whispered, his eyes burning with anticipation. "But he's calling for his horse to be brought round, so if we want to stop him leaving we need to move now."

"How many others?"

"Ten soldiers and several servants."

We all looked at each other. This time I was sure Evelyn was blaming herself for her injury.

"Maybe we should try to sneak out to the stables. We could find horses and try to beat him back to the castle." I suspected

110

that both Miles and Jake were looking for a fight, but I hated the idea of Miles going back into danger.

"But what about Evelyn?" asked Jake. "She can hardly ride a horse with a wound like that. And we can't leave her here unprotected. No, we have to stop him now."

I could read the truth in his eyes. After all this time, he wasn't leaving without confronting his cousin. I sighed.

"What do you think, Miles? Can we take those odds?" asked Jake.

The two men exchanged a calculating look.

"If their level of training is the same as the ones we just fought, we can do it," said Miles.

"Just make sure you don't do any permanent injury to any of the servants," said Jake. "They're not mercenaries like the soldiers, and they're not following Anhalt by choice."

Miles nodded his agreement, but I could read the concern in his eyes. It certainly complicated matters.

Jake carefully transferred Evelyn's weight on to my shoulder, and both men told us to wait in the corridor. Then they turned and rushed into the entrance way.

Immediate sounds of fighting broke out. I didn't even need to meet Evelyn's gaze to know she felt the same way I did. There was no way we were staying out here.

Moving slowly, I helped her to hobble toward the now open doorway. We paused at the threshold to take in the scene before us. Jake and Miles' momentum had carried the fighting away from the door. They were battling hard in the center of the entryway. The servants had all disappeared, and I was glad they were safe.

Evelyn said something to me, but I couldn't hear her over the echoing sounds of the fight. I followed her gaze and saw that she had spotted Anhalt lurking near the castle door. He looked bemused but not really concerned. He obviously felt he had enough soldiers present to subdue Miles and Jake.

With unspoken agreement, we began to make our way around the edges of the room. It was hard going with no one but me to support Evelyn, but slowly we made progress. I tried to keep my eyes in front of me, but they kept being drawn back to the fight in the middle of the room.

Every time a sword got near Miles, I gasped, and I could almost feel Evelyn rolling her eyes. I kept resolving not to do it and then, only a moment later, it would escape me again. I tried biting my tongue, but then I nearly tripped over a decorative suit of armor. After that, I stopped worrying about it and returned my attention to our own progress.

No one seemed to have noticed us, and we made it all the way to the front doors without incident. We were standing not far behind Anhalt now, but his eyes were locked on the battle in front of him. As his soldiers fell, one by one, his expression lost most of its confidence. When there were only two left fighting, he took a hurried step back.

Evelyn and I exchanged a look of determination. Carefully balancing on my shoulder, she reached down and retrieved the knife that she had returned to her boot.

Before I realized what she was intending, she pushed off from me and attempted to throw herself toward Anhalt. When her weight came down on her wounded leg, however, she crumpled. Instinctively throwing out her hands to catch herself, the knife went sailing out of her grip and slid across the floor.

I froze, expecting Anhalt to turn and see Evelyn lying practically at his feet, but instead his focus was fixed on the far side of the hall.

At the exact same moment as Evelyn's blade had hit the stone floor, the door across the room had burst open. A stream of people poured in.

For a moment, I thought they were more soldiers. Many of them were carrying swords, but it only took a minute to realize these weren't trained mercenaries. These were the castle servants. Obviously the ones who were in the entryway before had gone to fetch them.

They swarmed around Miles and Jake, forming a barrier between them and Anhalt. The two men tried to fight them off but were overwhelmed by sheer numbers, hampered as they were by their desire not to permanently injure a bewitched servant.

My eyes flew back to Anhalt, whose smile had returned, and then to the knife lying on the floor some distance away. I realized that the sight of Anhalt made me feel more sick than the weapon. I threw myself across the room.

Diving at the knife, I felt my hand close around the handle.

"Evelyn!" I screamed and slid the knife back across the floor toward her.

She turned just in time and caught the handle as it slid past her. Lunging up, all her weight on her good leg, she stabbed toward Anhalt.

He staggered backwards, clutching at his chest, but there was no wound there. For half a second I thought Evelyn had missed. And then I realized that she had caught the tip of the blade in one of the links of his golden chain. As she ripped downward, the metal snapped and the jewel fell, striking the stone floor hard with a loud ringing sound. It bounced slowly into the air, baleful shafts of red light flashing from its spinning facets.

The scene seemed to freeze before me. Anhalt, still clutching at his chest, stared at the gem in shock. The sound had somehow rung out above every other sound in the hall, and the fighters had all frozen, several in mid-swing.

Almost in unison, the servants wheeled around to stare toward the red stone. Then, one by one, they lowered their weapons, gazing at each other in confusion.

"What's going on?" I could hear several of them asking each other.

Another cried, "My Lord!" and bowed to Jake.

Seeing that Miles and Jake were out of danger, I hurried toward

Evelyn who had fallen heavily onto her wounded leg. She was barely conscious when I reached her. I knelt beside her, grasping her hand.

"It worked!" I said. "How did you know it would?"

"I didn't." Her voice was faint. "But I had to try something."

I pulled her head into my lap and continued to talk to her, trying to prevent her slipping into unconsciousness. Jake appeared at my side, looking frantic with worry. He was soon barking orders to the milling servants. Red seeped freely from her bandage, and I bit the inside of my cheeks in concern.

Several hands lifted Evelyn from my lap, and Jake assured me that the man now issuing orders was the castle doctor. I wanted to go with them, but I also didn't want to push my newfound ability to handle blood and gore. Instead I looked around for Miles, wanting to make sure he was unharmed.

I had hardly begun looking when he pushed through the crowd.

"Where is he?" he asked, looking around.

"Where is who?" I felt exhausted, and my brain struggled to keep up with the events of the last few minutes.

"Anhalt," said Miles, still gazing around the hall.

I gasped, and my eyes flew to the place where the gem and chain had fallen.

"Look," I said. "The jewel is gone, too!"

Jake swore and ran out of the hall. Miles took off after him. I considered following them but couldn't think of any possible help I could be. I tried instead to calculate how many hours it had been since I'd slept. I couldn't seem to work it out. At last, I simply sat down where I stood.

The men returned looking grim.

"His horse is gone," said Jake. "He got away. And I don't dare send any of my servants after him. He has the gem, and we don't know if its power was permanently destroyed or if it was only this enchantment."

"I'll go," said Miles. My heart contracted.

To my relief, Jake shook his head in a swift refusal.

"He could have gone in any direction, you'd never be able to find him alone. Plus, it's already dawn, and you haven't slept all night. I couldn't possibly let you go racing off into the forest."

Miles looked disappointed but didn't try to argue.

"I'm going to see what order I can bring to this chaos," said Jake. "I'll send a messenger to the queen right away, and then I'm going to check on Evelyn."

I wanted to say that I would go with him, but when I opened my mouth, nothing came out. I wondered if you could lose your voice to fatigue.

Jake strode off before I could remember how to form words, and I was left sitting on the floor next to Miles.

He looked down at me, and his eyes became intent. Suddenly my exhaustion faded, and my nerves began to glow instead. He reached down and pulled me to my feet. Slowly he led me over to a secluded corner of the hall.

"You've put me off several times now, and I'm not letting you do it again," he said, his voice firm.

I shook my head. "I don't know what you want to say exactly, but I do know that you're the son of the most powerful noble at the Rangmeran court and I'm the daughter of a traveling merchant. So, whatever it is, I think it would be best if you didn't say it."

"Best for whom, exactly?" he asked, looking down at me fondly.

"Best for my heart," I said, my words barely a whisper.

He grinned. I had seen his eyes blaze several times in the last few hours but never quite like this. The force of his expression made me catch my breath. I began to tremble.

He took me in his arms and gazed hungrily down into my face.

"I guess it's good that I don't want to say anything at all, then," he said. "I want to do this."

He crushed me against him and pressed his lips down over mine. The room spun around me, and I clutched at his jacket for support. He responded by pulling me even closer and deepening the kiss. I abandoned any thought of protest and returned his embrace enthusiastically.

"We've tracked him as far as the Northhelmian border," said the captain of the guard, "but I'm afraid he's long gone." From his expression, he was taking Anhalt's escape personally.

Hans sighed. "It's not good news, but it's hardly surprising."

Ava shook her head. "My godmother warned me that a darkness was coming to Northhelm—I just hope we're not the ones to have unleashed it. I'll have to send a diplomatic envoy to their king, of course. Not how I had been hoping to open diplomatic relations with them."

I wasn't in my normal place behind Ava's chair because my healing leg still wouldn't allow me to stand for long periods of time. Instead, I'd been given a seat at the table, along with Sarah, Miles, and Jake. I glared down at the lump of the bandage. If I hadn't been such an idiot and allowed myself to get wounded, I could have stopped Anhalt before he escaped.

Ava and Hans didn't blame me. In fact, they credited me with saving the day, and they'd refused to consider my resignation. Not that I would be back on duty for weeks.

I still blamed myself, though.

When the meeting broke up, Ava stopped Sarah with a question. I took the opportunity to hobble past her and catch Miles just outside the door. Since I'd woken up in Jake's castle, the two of them had been almost inseparable, and I'd been waiting for an opportunity like this for a while.

"Miles."

He turned and smiled at me. "How's the leg?"

"Healing," I said, not wanting to be distracted from my purpose. "I need to talk to you."

"Let me guess," he said, with a grin, "it's about Sarah."

"You two have been very close since we were all kidnapped," I said, watching his face closely. "The whole court is talking about it."

He shrugged his shoulders. "Let them talk."

"And your father? Are you equally unconcerned about his opinion?"

"My father doesn't control me," he said, still calm, "I make my own decisions. I was the one to help take Anhalt down, not him, after all."

"That's good to know," I gave him a long, level look. "And you should know that if you ever hurt her, I'll hurt you."

I was serious, but I could see he was, too, and I couldn't resist a small smile. "Of course, I've seen you fight now, so that's only if I can."

He smiled back at me. "I can assure you, if I ever hurt Sarah, I would let you beat me. As many times as you liked."

I nodded, satisfied. "Well, in that case, I wish you joy. I'm quite certain she'll run rings around you."

He laughed. "I'm pretty sure she's determined to run rings around us all."

Sarah emerged from the meeting room and cast a suspicious look between us.

"What's so funny?" she asked.

"Nothing," I said, a chuckle in my voice, "nothing at all."

She looked like she was about to press the matter further, but Miles captured her arm and began to lead her down the hall.

"Leave your poor cousin alone," I could hear him saying to her. "She's still recuperating."

I shook my head at his brazenness.

"They seem like a good couple," said a voice behind me.

I turned and smiled at Jake.

"I think they are," I said.

We began to walk slowly down the corridor in the opposite direction to Sarah and Miles. Jake matched his pace to mine without ever appearing impatient. I appreciated that about him. In fact, I appreciated a great deal about him. He kept appearing at my side, ready for a chat or just to sit in silent companionship. He'd only just received his proper title, but he apparently had plenty of time to keep me company as I recovered my strength.

"Hans just told me you tried to resign. I can't imagine why. I thought you liked your job as a guard," he said.

I examined his face but could see no sign of judgment. He seemed merely curious.

I shrugged uncomfortably.

"I do," I said. "But Ava is still establishing herself as queen. She needs the best. It only took a week for her and Hans to see the job was too much for me."

Jake shook his head. "You need to stop blaming yourself for not being able to do everything, Evelyn. It's not weak to need help. Having a strong team around you is a strength, not a weakness. Surely you learned that when you were guarding the caravan."

I considered his words. He was right about the caravan. Merchant guards were only as strong as their weakest member. My old Guardsmaster had drilled that into us often enough. We operated as a single unit, and it was why Caravan Hargrove was the safest caravan in the Four Kingdoms.

"It's different here, though," I said. "Here it's up to the personal guard to protect the queen."

"Certainly," he agreed, as calm and cheerful as ever. My heart sank a little at his words. Part of me had wanted him to keep arguing.

"But you know, traditionally," he continued, "the personal guard of a Rangmeran monarch is made up of a team of six guards who take rotating shifts."

I turned my head to stare at him.

"But Ava only ever had Hans when she was a princess."

He nodded. "Normally, as the daughter of the king, she would have had a team of three to guard her. But no one else would take the job. And Hans was so dedicated that eventually everyone sort of forgot there were supposed to be others. I think it's fairly obvious now why he was so single minded."

He smiled at me, and I let myself smile back. I felt like an explosion had gone through my brain. Why had I not known that about the monarch's personal guard? The answer was simple. I had spent my whole life in a merchant caravan, I knew nothing about how royal guards functioned.

Jake stopped and turned me to face him. His hands lingered on my arms, and I could feel warmth expanding out from where he touched.

"No one thinks you're weak for being injured or for needing us to fight for you. Neither Miles nor I could have done it on our own, either. In fact, you're the one who saved us by breaking the enchantment. And you just about killed yourself in the process. It's time you stopped trying to be a one-woman army and let some of the guards here help you."

I took a deep breath and nodded my agreement. An invisible load lifted off my shoulders. I didn't have to do everything, I just had to do my best as part of a team. That was easy—I had been training for that for years in the caravan.

We started walking again, and I couldn't keep the smile off my face.

"I'm glad to see that smile back," said Jake once we made it out into the sunshine. "I've been missing it."

I raised my eyebrows and he laughed.

"No, truly, I have. And I think you should enjoy every minute you have left as a personal guard."

"What's that supposed to mean?" After his previous words, I was pretty sure he was jesting, so I playfully bumped my shoulder into his.

"Oh, merely that I have every intention of convincing you to take up a different position just as soon as I can."

I stared at him, confused. "What do you mean?"

He looked at me and laughed. "Let's just say the position I have in mind is a little higher ranked than personal guard."

When I still didn't understand, he just watched me, his eyes smiling warmly into mine.

After a moment, his meaning burst on me, and I felt my whole body flush with warmth.

"But I...I..." I sputtered, wondering where my usual poise had gone.

A full smile broke across his face, and he tucked my hand into his arm.

"Don't worry," he said as he led me slowly onward, "you'll come around."

NOTE FROM THE AUTHOR

To find out what happens in Northhelm, read Marie's story, told in the third book in the Four Kingdoms series. Turn the page for a sneak peek of *The Princess Pact: A Twist on Rumpelstiltskin.*

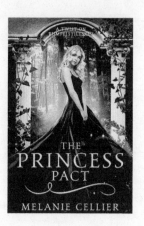

Thank you for taking the time to read my book. If you enjoyed it, please spread the word! You could start by leaving a review on <u>Amazon</u> (or <u>Goodreads</u> or <u>Facebook</u> or any other social media site). Your review would be very much appreciated and would make a big difference to me!

To be kept informed of my new releases and for free extra content, including an exclusive bonus chapter of my first novel, *The Princess Companion* (Book One of The Four Kingdoms series), please sign up to my mailing list at www.melaniecellier.com. At my website, you'll also find an array of free extra content.

FEAR

*T*he dark forest was rushing by so fast she couldn't make out details of the individual trees. She tried to pump her legs faster, but the bundle in her arms hampered her movements. She clutched it more tightly and risked a glance over her shoulder.

She wasn't looking for help. She had already made that mistake once before. She had thought then that a godmother might come to her aid, but a monster had come instead. The very same nightmare that now pursued her.

Pain was shooting up and down her legs, and her mouth ached from the cold air she gasped into her exhausted lungs. Fear could only push her body so far, and she had nearly reached her limit.

Just when she thought she would collapse, a dark figure loomed in front of her. She screamed, swerving and falling to the ground. She twisted as she fell in order to protect her burden and landed hard against an outstretched root.

She instantly recognized the silhouette in front of her, and her thoughts rushed back to the small attic room three years ago.

She could feel the rough straw in her fingers and see the dawn threatening through the windows.

And then the glint from the gold that was nothing compared to the avaricious gleam in the eyes of the man who kept her company. She had distrusted him even then, but she had been desperate for help from wherever she could get it. And she had been sure, with the bold certainty of youth, that she would find a way around his bargain.

And so the pact had been made.

"Why do you flee from me?" he asked. His voice had lost none of its arrogant assurance. "There really is no point, you know. You can't possibly escape me. A bargain is a bargain."

She looked down at the precious baby in her arms who was somehow still asleep.

"I'll be coming for her," he said, "when the time is right. So keep a careful eye out for me."

She woke, her eyes springing open and her heart racing, his incongruous high-pitched giggle echoing through her mind.

It was just a dream. It was just a dream, she told herself, but the terror lingered.

She knew that it wasn't just a dream. It was a warning. One day he would come, and he would claim what was his.

A pact is a pact, after all.

CHAPTER 1

*P*rincess Marie Christina Adrienne Camille of
Northhelm was bored. She did her best to keep an
expression of dutiful interest on her face, but inside she was sigh-
ing. The council meeting had already been going for two hours,
and the current discussion on trade regulations couldn't have
been more dull.

She knew that Northhelmians were famous for their careful
attention to detail, and she even knew it was a strength—one that
kept her kingdom in peace and prosperity. But ever since she had
returned from her visit to the neighboring kingdom of Arcadia,
she couldn't quite suppress her restlessness.

Several times she had been forced to restrain herself from
asking some particularly serious courtier if they had ever just had
fun. She could imagine the shocked look she would receive, and
the stories that would immediately circulate about the flighty
princess. So far, she had managed to keep the words from
tumbling out, but she was sure that one of these days she was
going to slip up.

For the past hour, her attention had been focused on the
empty chair across the table. Her brother usually filled it, but he

had complained to her earlier in the day that the agenda looked unusually tedious. And now his chair sat suspiciously empty.

She had spent the last sixty minutes trying to guess what excuse he had used for his absence. As the minutes ticked by, her ideas became more and more outrageous, so she was confident her brother had used none of them. The heir to the throne of Northhelm took his position with the seriousness and diligence it demanded.

Which meant he must have come up with something truly inspired.

Marie gave up trying to guess the excuse and allowed herself to focus on the most important aspect of the situation: his betrayal of his own sister. William should have known that the sibling code required her inclusion in his brilliance. Surely his excuse could have been stretched to cover them both.

She gave another internal sigh because she knew perfectly well that her brother would charm himself back into her good graces within minutes. She had always had a soft spot for him, and he was well aware of it.

Just as she was trying to harden herself toward him in preparation, the double doors to the council room flew open with such force that they hit the walls with a loud bang.

Read on in *The Princess Pact: A Twist on Rumpelstiltskin*

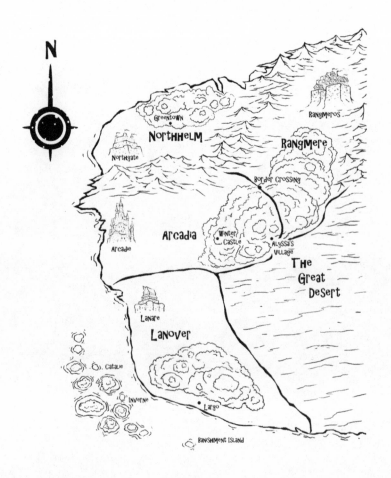

ACKNOWLEDGMENTS

This novella started as two short stories, but it wasn't happy to stay there. Sarah and Evelyn needed their own happily ever afters, and I had a lot of fun writing them.

As always, a big thank you to everyone who helped this story along. In particular:

My beta readers: Ber, Deborah, Katie, Priya, Rachel, Greg, and Rachel—you guys are the best!

My editors: Lyn and Dad—sorry for any mistakes I managed to introduce after you returned the manuscript to me.

My cover artist: Karri from Art by Karri—thanks for producing a cover that managed to so well convey both Sarah and Evelyn.

My family: Marc, Adeline, Mum, Dad, and everyone else (you know who you are!) for encouraging and supporting me through this journey and this story. I love you all madly.

And a final thanks to God for sustaining me through everything life throws my way.

ABOUT THE AUTHOR

 Melanie Cellier grew up on a staple diet of books, books and more books. And although she got older, she never stopped loving children's and young adult novels.

She always wanted to write one herself, but it took three careers and three different continents before she actually managed it.

She now feels incredibly fortunate to spend her time writing from her home in Adelaide, Australia where she keeps an eye out for koalas in her backyard. Her staple diet hasn't changed much, although she's added choc mint Rooibos tea and Chicken Crimpies to the list.

She writes young adult fantasy including her *Spoken Mage* series, and her *Four Kingdoms* and *Beyond the Four Kingdoms* series which are made up of linked stand-alone stories that retell classic fairy tales.

Made in the USA
Monee, IL
03 December 2021